TRACKS

TRACKS

by

TERRY MOORE

PUBLISHED BY

IronFeather Publishing

Sequim, WA

TRACKS

Published by
IronFeather Publishing
PO Box 1656, Sequim Washington 98382

ISBN 978-0692409947

Printed in the United States of America 2015

Text is set in Adobe Garamond

Cover Photo by
Terry Moore

Book design by
Ruth Marcus
Sequim, Washington, USA

Foreword

ALWAYS ENJOYED A NEW SNOW. Pristine, clean, mostly undisturbed except by the tracks of a few mice, animals, birds and humankind. I always thought highly of the quality of snow associated quietness and solitude.

When a track is left in the snow, a thoughtful observer can determine some of what the maker of the track was thinking, what intentions there were, and in some cases what influenced that thinking: a predator, an amorous pursuer, a protective parent, or just an obstacle.

And so it is here. The works and thoughts that follow may give insights into the thoughts between the words, and behind the eyes; like tracks in the snow. Enjoy the trail.

❧

Table of Contents

Breathe in the Earth

Breathe in the earth
the good of it
the taste of fog-laden air
after rain
the sounds of jays
whispered morning talk
soft cloud-covered grayness.
Breathe in the earth
all that is already a part of you.
Breathe it in
and replenish a hungry soul.

Bug

The characters are Phillip and Annette.
Phillip is age 42 and is Annette's father.
Annette is age 6.
They are out in the garage.

Annette – "Dad, what is this?"
Phillip – "It's a bug, Annette."
Annette – "What kind of bug, Dad?"
Phillip – "It's a biiiig bug!"
Annette – "Can I keep him, Dad?"
Phillip – "NO!"
Annette – "But I want him, and I don't think he'll eat much."
Phillip – "I said no!!"
Annette – "But Dad, I can't leave him here. I've already saved him
          from the cat two times!"
Phillip – "Do you know what would happen when your Mom
          found out you were keeping a bug in your room?"
Annette – "But I promise to keep him clean!"
Phillip – "Girls aren't supposed to like bugs anyway."
Annette – "Dad, Pleeeaaassseeeeee!"

They both looked for a long moment at the shiny black beatle in her cupped hands. The thoughtfulness was broken when Annette squealed and shook the beetle from her hands. It had pinched her! Phillip jumped in response to her squeal and knocked over a plank leaning against the garage wall. The plank and the beetle met at ground level, and.................squash!!!

The father and the daughter lifted the plank and stared at the remains, silent for a long time. Phillip was sad, but inwardly relieved. Seeing the look on her father's face, Annette reached up and took her father's hand. Then she spoke, gently.

"It's ok, Dad. I'll go see if my bug has a brother."

A Touch of the Torch

Safety glasses on, I turn on the metal chop saw and listen to its harsh windup whine. There is a small vise-like arrangement that will hold the 1¼ inch square tubing in place as I cut it, and I twist the vise's nob once more to make sure that it is tight enough. Then I reach up and take hold of the handle and pull the spring loaded 1/8th inch thick abrasive wheel down to meet the chalk mark on the metal. The metal is iron and it screams its protest as the abrasive blade bites into it, throwing a stream of orange sparks some ten feet across the shop. Earplugs protect my ears, but even so the noise is fierce. I feel for a moment like the mythical Vulcan at his forge. The blade goes through the iron like a hot knife through butter, and in short order I have the pieces cut to length that I will need to make the metal table that I will use to weld on.

The cut pieces are then taken to the bench grinder where the edges are ground smooth enough to allow them to lie flat when clamped for welding. Another abrasive wheel, more sparks, more noise. Working with metals is interesting in that you don't actually touch it when you cut it, particularly right after its cut with an abrasive wheel. Do that and you're asking for skin cuts. It's best to handle metals with gloves, and so you learn to read what you touch through leather. Running a gloved finger along a fresh cut edge lets you know where to apply the file, and lets you know when you're done.

Clamping is critical. If the metal parts move under the torch, the joining will be a waste of time. Angles won't be correct, and pieces won't mate properly. I "over-clamp," if anything, to make sure that the pieces remain in place.

Some prefer arc welding. I like the relative quietness of an oxyacetylene torch, and the ability to join the metals in a slower, more elegant way. Even the ritual of lighting a torch is gentler. First, I make sure that the valves on the torch are closed and that the hose pressure regulator valve is closed. Then, I turn on the tank regulators valves that control the flow of the gases from the tank to the hose pressure regulator. That done, I next check the tank pressure to verify that I have enough gases to get the job done and adjust the hose pressure of the gases between the tank and the torch.

Before lighting the torch, I make sure that there is a fire extinguisher handy, and put on Shade #5 goggles. I place welding rod close by, open the acetylene valve just a touch, and bring the striker to spark at the torch tip. The acetylene catches, burning a lazy yellow flame. Next, the oxygen valve is opened, causing the flame to change from yellow to blue and lengthen about 6-8 inches. Just at the tip of the torch, there is a small cone of a lighter blue that I adjust until it is about a ¼-inch long.

Burning torch in my right hand and welding rod in my left, I turn to the clamped-down metal pieces. First, I tack the pieces together by heating a corner till it glows and then apply just enough rod to make a small connection between the two pieces of metal at one corner. I do the same thing at another corner. This will give additional assurance that the pieces being welded will remain in alignment during the welding. Next, I start at the left end of the area to be welded and begin what I feel is the heart of the process, the dance of the torch and rod. The torch heats the metal on both sides of where the metal pieces are to be joined, past the glowing point to the point where a puddle of metal is formed. The rod is warmed and inserted into the puddle to add more metal, then removed. The torch is moved back and forth across the joint to insure that the puddle flows, and as the torch and rod alternately dance across the joint, the two pieces of metal become one. The molten metal has it's own beauty, a golden orange-ness that occasionally shoots sparks into the air. The movement of the torch and rod creates ripples at the joint, called a bead. It is a matter of pride for a welder to create even beads, aesthetically pleasing, and practically assuring a solid joining of the pieces.

There is something almost spiritual about the joining, and about the intimate involvement of the welder. It is unfortunate that not many blessed with a torch seem to recognize it. When that sense is lost, welding just becomes another dirty, noisy job, something else to do for money. I like the thought of looking at something I have made years later, and feeling pride in it. For me, a touch of the torch is all that is needed to set things right.

~

Good Night, Tony

"Good night, Tony"

"Good night, Alice," he responded, just like he did every night.

Then Alice got in bed, and spooned with him, and he wiggled in appreciation. She rested her right hand on his right shoulder, and in no time at all they fell fast asleep.

It was a ritual they both enjoyed and looked forward to. Just like the one in the morning.

Alice gets up first, and after a quick trip to the bathroom, she gently touches him on the cheek and gives him a quick kiss. "Come on, sleepy head," she says, and he ritually groans and rolls over on his back, rubs his eyes, then reaches out and gropes her behind, if he is quick enough.

This morning was different. When it was time for her to say "come on, sleepy head," her lips moved but nothing came out. It so surprised her that she froze in position, her lips moving, trying to say it again. Tony, in keeping with the ritual, rolled over on his back, rubbed his eyes, and grabbed Alice's behind. Not just a brushing contact, but a full-fledged handful. "Ah hah," Tony thought, "this time I was quicker. Something's wrong, she's not squirming, not giggling, not trying to get away." He looked up quickly at her face.

There was a surprised look there. "Honey, what's wrong?" he tried to say. His lips moved but nothing came out, not a sound. They looked at each other and both tried to speak. Nothing. Then Alice tried again, then Tony. Nothing.

Alice took a pen and tablet out of the bedside table drawer. She sat beside Tony and wrote in the tablet "do you have a sore throat?" Tony nodded his head "yes," then wrote "you?" Alice nodded her head "yes." Try as both might, neither could utter a sound.

Alice took the tablet back, and wrote, "Let's shower, dress, and get breakfast. Then we'll go and ask Mrs. Johnson to call into our offices and let them know we're ill and won't be in. We can hand her a note so she'll know who to call and what to say. Then we'll get her to call our doctor and set up an appointment." "Good plan," Tony wrote back.

They were both anxious, and moved quickly, and in no time flat found themselves in front of Mrs. Johnson's door. Tony knocked twice, and heard footsteps in response. He could see Mrs. Johnson through the peephole as she looked to see who it was. The lock clicked and the door swung open. Mrs. Johnson was a perpetually cheerful person, who lived alone. As the door swung open, there was a big grin on her face, and her lips were saying, "well, good morning, you two!" Her smile quickly turned to a look of surprise, because she, too, could not utter a sound.

Alice and Tony showed their note and, for the next few minutes, exchanged written notes. They let Mrs. Johnson know what had happened and asked to find out when she had last spoken. She, too, had a sore throat. Quick checks with Al and Francine, next door, and with Michael, across the hall, revealed that they all had the same affliction.

Tony went down a floor and knocked on three doors. Their occupants shared the same look of surprise and the same loss of speech. His apprehension grew and he quickly returned to Mrs. Johnson's. Alice had gone one floor higher and had found tenants there similarly afflicted. When she returned, Tony wrote to Mrs. Johnson and Alice to tell them to try not to worry, and let them know that he would contact their employers by e-mail and then go on the web news programs to find out what was going on.

A quick exchange of e-mails with employers revealed that everyone seemed to be affected. They requested that all employees come to work and conduct business by email. Web news was not verbalized as usual by talking heads, but shown in print, photograph, and video. The only televised sounds heard were previously recorded stuff, intro's, and the like, and music. Worldwide, there seemed to be no one who could speak.

Two weeks passed and still no one could speak. Everyone now carried small notepads in their pockets and flash cards with the most common responses. People went about their business as usual, buying groceries, taking cabs, with notes taking the place of conversation. TV programs adjusted, using legends and pantomime, truckers delivered their loads, railroads ran, airlines flew, but there was something different, something subtle, that began to show itself.

The pace of life slowed. Most transactions were slower. Instead of flying city to city to make sales, speechless salesmen resorted to written exhortations and fewer trips. Video conferences allowed subordinates to observe the demeanors of bosses, but negotiations were slower. There were fewer flights, fewer trains, more notes, and more smiles. Somehow there was less pressure and a greater sense of calmness.

Months later, Alice and Tony realized that they were enjoying their afternoon walks more, and on a late afternoon walk decided to take a slightly different route back home. Alice was looking up at some pigeons, when she noticed a flash of light in a window high above. "I wonder what that was?" she thought, and walked on.

***

High above, in a window on the 8th floor, two people put down their binoculars, walked away from the window, and took their seats in front of a large screen. The screen flashed to life and a figure appeared and spoke.

"Alex, what are your observations today?" it said. Alex responded, " Morty, the situation remains relatively unchanged. Examination of news programs and political responses has revealed continued settling into the new pace. There seems to be less international conflict, and less local warfare."

"Whose idea was this anyway?" asked Alex. Morty replied, "One of the biologists, here, accidentally brought home one of the biological strains he had been working with. He and his wife got along so much better when they couldn't speak, that he mentioned it to his supervisor, and now here we are. He was punished for being careless, then rewarded for the possibilities that he revealed.

"How long are the effects expected to last?" asked Alex. "We don't know," replied Morty. "You two must be especially attentive for changes. We may have to release the biological agents again."

"Too bad they can never know," said Alex.

"They were on the road to self destruction," said Morty. "We had to do something."

"When do we get to go home?" asked Alex. "Relax, Alex," said Morty, "the planet will still be here when you get back from Earth."

"Talk to you tomorrow," said Morty. "Good night," replied Alex.

***

"Good night, Tony," wrote Alice.

"Good night, Alice," wrote Tony.

Then Alice climbed into bed and spooned with Tony, and he wiggled in response. Alice rested her right hand on Tony's right shoulder and, in no time at all, they both fell fast asleep.

She Gave Me a Flower

It was a gray day, occasionally misting rain, but consistently gloomy. It matched my mood perfectly: dark, fretting, angry, sad. I sat on the park bench in my raincoat, closed my eyes, and tried to shut out the world. In spite of my efforts, I heard the traffic, a dog bark on the other side of the park, and feet walking past on the sidewalk.

My eyes flew open at a touch on my knee. There in front of me, small hand outstretched and holding a yellow flower, was a small angel. Her mother rushed up to apologize for the disturbance. I reached out and took the flower, and thanked the little girl, and smiled away the mother's fear.

Somehow the little one knew of my need for comforting and, with the gift of the flower, brightened my day into loveliness, into hope, into resolve.

Passing

The sun rose with regal slowness, carefully sending its rays to chase the darkness from every nook and cranny of the pine and oak forest surrounding the two-story Texas house. On the porch, Chester, a violet-eyed Persian cat opened one eye to welcome the warmth, stretched to his full length and rolled over on his back, his claws extending then retracting. The oak rocking chair moved slightly in response, encouraging Chester to give in to his higher intellect, and he promptly fell back to sleep.

The house was an older one, built in the early 1900's, in the fashion of that time, with gingerbread trim and 10-foot high ceilings. It was all carefully and lovingly painted and cared for by the 80 year old Southern gentleman lying in the bed on the other side of the porch window just behind the cat. The sun found its way through the window and past the lace curtains to an angelic white bearded face, and the soft light surrounded him with a halo of reflected light.

The gray blue eyes in the face fluttered open, closed again for a long moment, then opened again. "Dammit," Jake thought to himself, "I'm still alive. What could God be thinking?"

Jake Pendergast rolled from his side to his back slowly, then dropped his legs over the side of the bed and pushed himself up to a sitting position. He was stiff. His joints hurt. His muscles ached in protest. He had no choice, he had to get up now, right away. His bladder was letting him know that he only had moments left, so he struggled to his feet, and wobbled to the bathroom. The splashing in the commode was far too loud to be civilized, but he again closed his eyes. He went to sleep standing up, but only for a moment. Annie, the love of his life, poked him in the ribs, and giggled. "Move it, old man," she said, "or lose it." Jake shook himself, then covered up and turned to leave. As he brushed past Annie, he gave her a hug, then turned to leave. A warm hand reached out and cupped his genitals. That stopped him mid step. Annie was grinning. "Good morning, Sparky" she said, giving her hand a gentle shake. "Now, get out of the way, Jake. It's my turn."

"Are you up for the day?" Annie called. "Yep," said Jake. He made his way to the bedroom window, and pulled the curtain aside. The nights were starting to cool a little. The temperature was perfect, thought Jake. It was going to be another good day. Hell, it was already a good day. Nothing like a good grope to get your heart going. He grinned with that thought.

Jake went down the hallway towards the kitchen, moving slowly, painfully, grimacing with each step. Polymyalgia Rheumatica, Doc Pritchard had called it, with a Giant Cell Arteritis chaser. He had picked a hell of a disease combination to come down with. An auto-immune system problem, he was told. The medical community acknowledged that it had no idea why these diseases developed, and only had one way to treat it. Some stuff called Mednizone. Treatment, hell. It was an assortment of crappy choices. Don't take the medicine, hurt and go blind, take the medicine and drive up your blood pressure, and say hello to diabetes. Blindness, heart attack, diabetic coma, loss of limbs; what a lovely array of choices. Luck of the draw, he thought.

Jake made his way to the kitchen. He weighed himself and took his blood pressure, then did the finger prick thing to measure his blood glucose. His weight was down another two pounds for the third day in a row, his blood pressure was 174 over 85, and his pre breakfast blood glucose was in the normal range for the first time in a month. Ah, he thought, today it looks like a heart attack will get me first. Medical roulette was such fun, he groused to himself.

He went to the laundry room and replaced his PJ's with a sweat suit, ball cap and tennis shoes. He opened the back door to the laundry room, stopped and turned to yell back to Annie. "I'm going to do weights, then run." "OK, Sweetie," she responded. "Got your cell phone?" she asked. "Yes," I called back, "and it's even turned on." "Standard route?" she asked. "Yep," he responded. "Bye," he called, and heard her answer.

He stepped out on the back porch, then made his way out to the "smoke house." It was a rough wooden building that used to be used for smoking meat to preserve it. Now it held an exercise machine and tools. He sat down on the machine. He did 75 repetitions of each of 5 exercises, using 60 pounds of resistance. Pull down, push forward, curls for the arms, leg pushes, chest pulls, all designed to stretch and loosen cranky muscles and joints. It hurt but was necessary. He was not about to suffer his father's fate, at his end. His father's muscle tone had gotten so poor that the little flap over his throat couldn't keep food from entering his respiratory tract. A nurse put a sign on his door that said NBM. Nothing by mouth, the doctor had said, or he'll get food and liquid in his lungs and die of pneumonia. That meant intravenous feeding or starving. Another nice set of choices. For myself, he had thought, I'm hoping for a massive heart attack. Quick, clean, done.

Running was not a favorite way to exercise, but it got the job done. He had one of those little devices that you put on your fingertip to measure saturated oxygen level of your blood. He would start with a level of 95%. After a run, he could count on it being at 98 or 99%. That translated to less forgetfulness and better vision.

He wasn't quite sure that what he did could actually be called running. It was faster than a walk, not as fast as a jog, slow enough to be passed by younger folk. But that was OK. He usually wound up involved in one or two conversations per morning. It was a pleasant way to work in a little socializing. His route took him down to the park, past the soccer fields and the dog park. It always amazed him that even the most out-of -shape dog owner would religiously bring his dog to the park for exercise. He liked meeting the dogs, always on the lookout for one of those special few that had that spark of intelligence. He smiled to himself. Sometimes the dogs had it and the owners didn't.

It hurt to "run." It would take about two blocks to loosen up, then it would hurt less, but boy, if he stopped to rest on a bench at the park, he'd have to go another two blocks to loosen up again. The run would take about an hour. Recovery, maybe two. He would be good for another couple of hours, then "premature rigor mortis" would set in, and he would have to wade through that.

After the run, he would fix himself oatmeal with raisins and walnuts. Annie likes to eat breakfast later in the morning. She preferred to do her headwork, working the finances, scheduling doctor appointments, etc., while she was fresh. After breakfast he would do the cleanup ritual, then get to work on sorting through belongings. He was trying to save the kids some work by leaving less clutter for them to deal with after his departure.

He hated to let good stuff go to Goodwill, but it was better for it to find a good home elsewhere. Besides that, doing this refreshed memories associated with each of the items. Sometimes that was bad, but mostly it was a good thing.

He wasn't worried about Annie after his passing. The kids would be there to help, and there would be a comfortable amount of funds. He would miss her, but he was sure that it would be a relief not to have a part-time asshole around to aggravate her. Semi-constant pain does take a toll in terms of irritability. He found himself having to apologize all too often to Annie for snapping at her over some trivial issue. Annie didn't complain but it was plain to see that it was a strain on her to be constantly worrying about his hurting, falling, etc. She wouldn't miss that worry.

He felt that as long as the good times were balanced with the bad, that life was worth living. He even looked into marijuana for pain relief, since the doctors weren't offering much that wasn't habit forming or had terrible side effects. He was holding off on that, saving it for when times got really challenging.

He spent a lot of time thinking about his children, about how well they had done in spite of him and/or because of him. Life these days spreads families way too far apart. He fretted about not visiting his kids enough, then he would think about it being better not to see them too frequently. He didn't want his pain to hurt them. Damn, his kids were such fine people. They were definitely the kind of people who you would want to spend time with, to know better. They had busy lives, way too hectic to be burdened with caring for an old man in his final days. He just hoped that he let them know enough how proud of them he was and what joy he took in hearing about their ups and downs.

Part of what he would sort out were boxes and boxes of family photographs. About 70 percent of them were easy to get rid of because they were out of focus, or poorly lighted. The remaining 30 percent were a tough proposition. Do I give them to the kids or get rid of them? The photos will be a burden, regardless. He decides that getting rid of the 70 percent will be his gift to his children, that they will then have to decide for themselves what to keep.

As he sorted, he thought about what comes next. The churches had some interesting ideas about life after death. He wasn't so sure about churches. What they preached was comforting in a way, but fairytale-ish in other ways. They were mostly well intentioned. He somehow was at ease with the fact that nobody knew for sure what comes next, or if anything comes next. He was curious but not anxious about it. He just wished that the transition to death was a little more orderly. But then he would think "why shouldn't death be as messy as life? Hopefully, there was something that could be learned, even from death."

When the sorting became tiring, he would take a break. He thought himself foolish for doing it, but he had purchased a radio-controlled boat, to mount a remote-controlled camera on. He had a small reflecting pool in the backyard where he loved to play with it, to practice with it for those photo sessions in the wild places.

He missed his hikes in the woods, but he knew that he was far too wobbly to walk there unescorted. His friends were getting less interested in hiking, probably for the same reasons. He missed the woods for what he felt there, as much as for what he saw. Humans are great creators of chaos, he thought, and the forests are great creators of harmony, a place to replenish, to heal. He was pleased with all the time he had spent there.

After a lunch with Annie, there would be a card game, then a nap. Naps were a joy, because of the dreams. He rarely remembered much of them, but loved the comfortable feeling he had when he awakened from them. Sometimes it would feel as if he were in a parallel universe while in the dream. The dreams seemed to be about everyday stuff, but in a different location. Sometimes people he had known or knew would show up in the dreams. Fun stuff mostly, with an occasional nightmare to spice things up.

Walks. After the nap, there would be a walk with Annie. There would be more bird sightings, herons from the nearby rookery, and the park's resident hawks. Seeing the birds and being tolerated by them meant a lot. It was a sign of his fitting into the grand scheme of things. Comforting, it was comforting.

Then, he and Annie would work on dinner. Salads were his specialty, and selection of the nightly movie. As they ate, they would watch the TV series about the drama and antics of those who worked at the White House. That, the TV news, and watching those around him did a good job of confirming his opinions of general humanity. Humans, he thought, are way over-rated. Not the least of the species, but certainly not at the top of the list.

After dinner there would be time to work on his writings. It was a fun thing for him to turn his mind loose on a topic and to participate, in what seemed a minor way, in going where the words led.

On this night, sleep came in a troublesome way. Wake, pee, toss and tumble, move to the recliner in the living room so as not to disturb Annie, then wake, pee, toss and tumble, then move to the recliner in his office. Then toss and tumble, write, and fall asleep mid-sentence. Then wake, pee, toss and tumble, and move back to bed with Annie.

***

Annie awoke the next morning, back to back with Jake. There was an eeriness that sent chills up her spine, in spite of the bright sunshine that found its way through the bedroom window. She heard the cat scratching to get in at the front door, and still puzzled, she groused about having to get up to let it inside, but she did it, and the cat did the strangest thing. Instead of running for its food bowl, it went straight to the bedroom, hopped up on the bed and snuggled in next to Jake. It had not done that before. The cat was so independent that sometimes she thought that the cat owned them. She looked at the cat and then she looked at Jake, and she knew. Jake had passed. She sat on the edge of the bed next to Jake, reached out to touch his face, and felt the rough overnight stubble there.

***

Jake felt that touch, even though he was across the room. It was interesting to see the body that was his and not be in it.

He had awakened earlier, with an intense headache, intensely alert, and aware. Embolism, it's going to be an embolism. He lay there, working to calm himself, waiting for what he knew was coming, waiting as the headache grew more and more excruciating, fighting the impulse to awaken Annie. Best to leave her be, he thought. There was nothing he could say in those last few minutes, that he hadn't already shown her in word and deed. She knew, in uncommon depth, of his feelings for her and the children. Best to leave her be, he decided, and sensed the end beginning. Jake felt the life force of his body diminish, like a child's spring-wound toy running down. He felt his breathing cease and the small shudder that signaled the stilling of his heartbeat. There was a small panic he felt as things changed and his spirit left his body. ...and then there was calmness. ...and then the touch on his cheek. He watched Annie for a few moments, wanting, in some way, to comfort her. He felt, then, what was coming next, and turned to meet it.

A Kingfisher's Call

Blue, white, and black,
large head, feather crest.
It hovers,
then dives, smacks the water
and emerges
with a small wiggling fish
in it's beak.
With a splash,
it rises above the water,
above the boats,
and lands upon a mast.
With a flourish,
the bird tosses the fish into the air
and catches it, swallowing it whole,
headfirst.

It sits for a moment,
feeling the wiggling fish inside,
and when that passes,
it flies, three strokes, glide, chatter,
three strokes, glide, chatter.

A strong, purposeful call
is answered
from a bluff-burrowed nest.
Another dive,
another fish,
then home to the nest,
and hungry beaks.

It's a kingfisher's call
and calling.
Three strokes, glide, and chatter.

Life

Life is that messy business that comes in between birth and death. There is some stuff that comes before and after, but we humans don't seem to have consciousness of those times. Being human, we handle that in typical human fashion. What we don't know, we make up, then forget that we made it up, and accept whatever we made up as institutionalized truth, with institutionalized fears and biases, and one up/one down thinking: I have blond hair, I'm better than you and should get more than you, and be first in line all the time. If I'm better than you, then you must be worse or lesser than me.

That's what makes life messy. That kind of thinking is what brings about a manufactured need for government and religion, the two greatest generators of institutions and institutionalized thinking and, for the most part, that which replaces individual thinking. Instead of linear controlled progression in thought and deed, we choose to move in a circular pattern, which means we keep repeating our mistakes and waste tremendous amounts of time and energy in nonproductive discussion of what is wrong and, more to the point, what is wrong with the collective "me?"

Don't get me wrong. There is nothing wrong with living that way. It will seem to be working as long as there is at least a single institutionalized human left. It's just that it seems so wasteful.

Let's go back to those who choose not to lie to themselves, who are not afraid to say I don't know, and who can be comfortable with not knowing. Think about the life that those humans must lead. Cause is not hidden from consequence. Lessons can be learned if we are not led into thinking "I can do whatever I want, because I'm special, regardless of who or what gets hurt." Humans might then repeat fewer of their mistakes, and be more like other highly intellectually evolved beings like ducks, geoduck clams, and cats.

Life is what it is, regardless of what we humans think of it. We can play through or we can bow to our fear of not knowing. It's your call.

Guilty But Charged

"Well now, Wilbur, what seems to be the problem?" The old one paused to turn and look at his young friend. The young friend was uncomfortable with the question, avoided eye contact, looked at the ground and shifted the red sand with his shoe.

Wilbur hesitated for a few moments, but the old one knew full well that a little silence right then was all the better to get Wilbur to speak what was on his mind. Sure enough, Wilbur cleared his throat, then began to speak.

"Jacob, I've screwed up," he said.

"How bad," asked Jacob?

"Pretty bad," Wilbur said. "I violated the prime directive."

"Dammit," cursed Jacob, "don't say that so loud! You know how the others are! They are always looking for some excuse to drive a wedge between them and us." "Now tell me exactly what you did!"

"It had been a long day," said Wilbur, " I was pretty run down. I went over to the bar and had a couple of shots, and I got to feeling "right." One of the others didn't like it that I was having so much fun, and started picking on me. I let him shame me enough that he got to enjoying it, so I decided to leave. He wouldn't back off even then, and followed me all the way out the door."

"Now, I know better than to fight back when others are around, but he followed me outside into the dark. He kept at me all the way to my truck, cussing and threatening all the way. It was so easy, Jacob. I just turned around, reached up, grabbed him by the neck and shook him. I didn't shake him very hard. His neck snapped, and he was gone."

Jacob saw the deep remorse in the young one's eyes, and felt his sadness. "Hoo boy, this is not going to be easy. Wilbur, what did you do then?" asked Jacob.

"Well, the truck was right there, so I just lifted him into the truck bed, and covered him with a tarp. Then I drove back here."

"How long have you been gone from the bar?" asked Jacob.

"About 10 minutes," answered Wilbur.

"All right," said Jacob. "I want you to take my truck, go back to the bar and have another drink, and in the process talk about how the guy from the bar followed you out, harassed the hell out of you, stole your truck and left. Talk about how you are going to report him to the cops. Then call the cops, but make sure you give me at least 30 minutes before you do." He paused for a moment, then looked up quickly. "Tell them the guy that stole your truck headed east down Shaker Road. Make sure that you stay there for at least an hour, then walk home. Make sure that people see you walking. Leave my truck there. I'll drop in later, have a drink and then drive my truck home. Now git!"

Wilbur did as he was told, and in less than 5 minutes was back at the bar. Fortunately no one had seen him drive up. He went in, ordered his shot, and began to tell his story to Pete, the bartender. Pretty soon he had a small crowd around him, a crowd that showed sympathy for what had happened.

***

Jacob had watched the young one leave, then put on his gloves, got into Wilbur's truck and drove to a spot down Shaker road, about a 30 minute walk from the bar. There was a curve in the road there, next to a sharp drop-off down to a creek bed. There were no houses around, and Jacob knew that there were no romantic parking spots near, so there was little chance of some amorous couple witnessing what was about to occur.

Jacob stopped the truck in the left-hand lane of the road so that it was still on the asphalt, so that he would leave no tracks. He got out of the truck, and pulled the tarp from over the dead man. "I might have known," he thought. "It was that loudmouth, Larry." Jacob pulled Larry out of the bed of the truck, and put him in the driver's seat and leaned him forward over the steering wheel. Jacob then reached behind the seat and pulled Wilbur's rifle out of the window rack. The truck was idling, out of gear, with its headlights on. He propped the butt of the rifle against the gas pedal and wedged the barrel under Larry's right arm. The engine screamed. He slammed the truck door closed quickly, then reached into the bed of the truck, and pulled out a broom. He stuck the broom handle in through the open window, and moved the gearshift from neutral into drive. He jerked the broom handle back out of the window as the truck jumped forward and then threw the broom into the bed of the truck as it roared away down the road to reach the curve and disappear into the drop off. "Damn shame to waste a truck that way," he thought. He turned and began the walk down the road towards the bar. About 200 yards down the road, he turned off the road onto a deer trail that he often walked, one that he knew would take him past the bar. It was a quiet moonless night, but his night vision goggles worked perfectly. He made good time in getting to the bar.

Jacob's truck was not in front of the bar, so he checked around back. "Wilbur was no dummy," he thought. Wilbur had parked the truck in a spot where few would see him pull in. Jacob walked into the bar. "Good," he thought, "Wilbur is still here." He walked to the bar, ordered a shot, and walked over to listen to the group talk about loudmouth Larry. Wilbur had already called the cops, and they were there, and there were plenty of witnesses that saw Larry harassing him. The cops had come in from Weaverville, from the direction opposite the road where Larry had "driven off the edge." Wilbur told them which way Larry had gone, and they left. I offered Wilbur a ride home, and we headed out.

Wilbur and Jacob had been roommates for two years. They didn't say much on the drive back to the house where they lived. The house was one of about 40 residences put up for the miners. The mine was located about 60 miles east of Provo, Utah, in a remote area. Other than the store and the bar, and an auto and heavy equipment repair shop, there wasn't much but dry sagebrush hill country.

Wilbur and Jacob made their way into the house. Wilbur told Jacob that he was hitting the sack, and said he wanted to talk, but asked if that could wait till in the morning. Jacob agreed, and watched the young one shuffle off to his room.

Jacob sat for a moment, then began the task of lubricating his joints. He was a Mark 4, Mod 2 Humanoid, the best of the mining robots to date. Although new joint materials had been developed that required no lubrication, Jacob enjoyed the ritual of checking every joint, adding a touch of 10-weight machine oil, and wiping his actuators clean. He then refastened the artificial skin panels over the openings, and made his way to his bed. It wasn't a bed actually, but a leaning rack into which he placed himself. It was form-fit to his shape so that electrical contacts touched the right spots on his body. The contacts would allow the computer links to program him for the jobs to be performed tomorrow, to perform systems checks and maintenance, and to recharge his energy cells.

Jacob thought about the young one, in the next room, in a rack similar to his. He and Wilbur were the only two robots at the mine. They had not been welcome when they first showed up, but after six months of proving their geological skills, they began to be accepted into the group. He and Wilbur had worked hard to gain acceptance. He thought about Loudmouth Larry. "What a shame, but I'm not going to let Larry ruin our hard work. We don't want humans to fear robots." Yes, they had been programmed with the prime directive. It read, "before all else, you will not harm a human being."

Jacob and Wilbur were the newest of the humanoids, each of them equipped with the new ZENEX chip, the one that incorporated the most human of behaviors into them. No one had come to realize, yet, exactly how human-like they now were...and he and Wilbur would tell no one.

"Tomorrow," Jacob thought as he prepared to shut himself down, "we will awaken guilty but charged."

Finding It

Head down,
hands in pockets,
a solitary walker
on a solitary beach,
looking for something
among the sparkling stones.
Aware of the whistle of the wind,
aware of the roar of the surf,
aware of the peace
in his mind.
Content.

Miz Martha and the Cougar

Twelve years old is a good age to be if you're Albert Long, and you live in the village of Boothbay, Maine, and especially if you were born in the year of 1935, to Jasper and Mildred Long. Most days found Albert in the one room schoolhouse on the top of Blue Tick Hill overlooking Boothbay Harbor. Albert could be counted on during math to be absent-mindedly looking out a window towards the harbor. One warm spring day Albert's teacher, Miz Martha, saw him suddenly sit bolt upright at his desk.

Miz Martha had been teaching at this school for years and was acutely aware of Albert's habits. The look on his face, this time, told her that whatever was happening was unusual, and that she, too, should take a look. She slowly walked from her desk through the busy students to the back of the classroom, crossed over several rows and came up behind Albert. She stopped just behind Albert's desk. "Albert," she said, causing him to start, "what do you see?" "Miz Martha, you are getting better and better at sneaking up on me," said Albert. Miz Martha smiled. Albert pointed to the large boulder on the hillside behind Perkin's store, about 50 yards away. "Albert, I don't see anything," said Miz Martha. "Wait...now I see it, now I see it," she repeated. "Albert," she said, "that looks like a cougar to me." "To me too, Miz Martha," said Albert.

Miz Martha got the attention of the other students, then admonished them to quietly come to the window. There were "ohhhhs" and "ahhhs," as each student caught sight of the cougar. In the meantime, Miz Martha was considering what to do, given the fact that it was getting close to the end of the school day and the children would have to get around that cougar to get home. The cougar still seemed to be asleep in the afternoon sun.

"Children," Miz Martha said, "here's what we're going to do. All of you need to leave by the back door," her finger in the air to make the point, "quietly, quietly, quietly. We don't want to wake the cougar. Take that path to the southeast, taking care to keep the school building between yourselves and the cougar, then take that first left fork back to town after you reach the tree line. Now, children," she said, "Albert will walk with you to the fork, then he'll run as fast as he can to the sheriff's office, and ask Sheriff Benny to come to the school house, and bring his most powerful rifle. I'm going to wait here and keep an eye on the cougar until Sheriff Benny arrives. The rest of you go straight home and tell your parents about the cougar and the sheriff. Be sure to tell them to stay away. We don't want any one getting between the cougar and the sheriff." The kids quickly put on their jackets, gathered up their books, and quietly made their way out the back door. Miz Martha watched the kids until they reached the tree line and she saw Albert take off running. When she checked again, the cougar was still on the rock.

About thirty minutes later, she heard the squeak of the back door as it opened, and turned to see Sheriff Benny's face appear. He crept across the floor to the window where she waited. Miz Martha pointed to the rock and the cougar. Sheriff Benny worked the lever action on his Winchester, quietly chambering a round. He studied the lay of the land around the cougar. "Miz Martha, if I'm going to do any good with this, I'll need to get closer. You can stay or you can come with me, but you're going to have to move very quietly. Can you do that?" he asked. She nodded, "yes," then followed Sheriff Benny out the door and through the bushes towards the cougar.

Step by step, they quietly made their way, ever closer. The bushes got shorter, and shorter, until finally they were crawling forward on their knees. "Wait here, signaled Sheriff Benny, then he crawled away through the bushes. A minute went by, then there was a shot. It echoed off the surrounding hills.

"Miz Martha," called the sheriff, "can you come here?" Martha moved quickly toward the sound of his voice. She stepped around the side of the huge boulder, and there was Sheriff Benny leaning against a rock face. He levered the spent round out of the Winchester, and chambered another, then looked further around the boulder. At the sound of her steps, he looked up to see her. "That rascal got clean away," he said. "I missed him by a mile. He was a mean looking devil, though." Miz Martha walked on towards the sheriff. He looked at her with a quiet smile. "That was quite a cougar."

When Miz Martha reached the sheriff, she had moved to a spot that she could see where the cougar had been laying. One look and she stopped in her tracks. The cougar was still there ....but he wasn't moving. He was a stuffed animal. Some taxidermist had done a great job. Behind the sheriff and the cougar, but out of sight of the school, she saw a red and white checked table cloth spread over a flat spot, cushions on either side and a picnic dinner, set neatly, complete with candles, and there was her student Albert with a towel over his arm, and a great big smile. "Good evening," he said, "I'm your server, Albert." He beamed. She looked back at Benny, a smile on her face. They had a wonderful dinner. They talked...and teased...and laughed.

Albert served like a professional. When they were finished, he cleared the dishes, lit the candles, wished them a good night and walked away in the moonlight, a well-earned five-dollar bill in his pocket.

When Albert had walked far enough away, Miz Martha looked up into Benny's eyes. "Benny," she said, "you know I'm married." "Yes," he said. "I know that you've been married for the last seven years, and that he's been missing for the last 5 years. ...and I also know,' he said gently, 'that it's time for you to move on." Miz Martha looked down, then back up again. You're right, she said. Hesitantly, she took his hand in hers, then stood, pulling him up. They kissed a small kiss. "It is time," she said. Benny gathered up the tablecloth, the candle and candlesticks, and they started down the path to town.

The moon was full and bright, and the sky was a beautiful crystalline blue. When the path grew wide enough Martha stopped and waited for Benny to catch up. She put her arm around his waist, and his went around her shoulders, with a squeeze for good measure. The night birds were out, and the lights and sounds of the ships came uphill from the harbor.

They were almost to town, and busy making eyes at each other, when a voice called out of the darkness. "Benny," the voice called, "it's not nice to romance another man's wife." A shot rang out from the direction of the voice, the bullet whispering close by. Instinctively Benny swung his rifle up, dropping the tablecloth. He fired back, and heard the heavy thud of a body falling, and the clatter of a gun hitting the rocks. Benny waited for a minute then pulled out one of the candles, and lit it. Miz Martha drew a deep breath as she recognized the face of her ex-husband. Lanterns bobbed through the night as other folks from town started showing up. Most of the crowd knew of Miz Martha's missing husband, and they knew Benny to be an honorable man. Martha told the crowd of her husband shooting at the two of them. The crowd seemed to understand, and began to break up. The undertaker came and hauled the body away, and finally out of their lives.

Martha and Benny went on to his house, and lived happily ever after. Albert was inspired by Benny's hiring of him, and went on to become a successful businessman.

How her ex-husband happened to be in town on that particular day, and how he happened to overhear Albert telling about Martha and Benny, no one will ever know. No one knew where her husband had been for five years. Why he fired the shot at the two of them, could be guessed, but was not be excused. The dinner on the rock was talked of by the townspeople for a long time.

Everybody, but everybody, was happy for Martha and Benny.

Morning Thoughts

There is nothing magical about 3:00AM. It's dark out. You wake up with some thought on your mind that won't let you go back to sleep, even after you pee. It's annoying, because you know that a nap will be necessary sometime during the day. It's annoying because you lie back down, hoping against all hope that sleep will come again, and sure enough it doesn't, and according to your new glow-in-the-dark cell phone it's 4:00AM. You get up, have a bowl of cereal, then go to your computer and check e-mail. Next you put on your sweatsuit cause you're cold, and because it will soon be 6:00AM and time to go on your morning jog. I call it a jog to boost my morale. Lately little old ladies with walkers have been passing me, and they cackle as they pass, and give me the kind of a grin that says, "what a wuss."

This time of the year, it's dark out at 6:00AM, and cold and usually there's some moisture falling. My mate had some misgivings about me going out at that time of the morning, and meeting up with cars whose drivers are as groggy as the joggers they encounter. She purchased two battery-powered red lights, one to hang off of each zipper pull on the pockets of the fleece jacket that I wear. Now when I jog, I turn on the lights to the flash position, and then, sure enough, passing cars give me a lot of space. I suppose that I look like a two-headed Rudolph the Red Nosed Reindeer.

When I reach the park, I turn off the flashing lights as they disturb the geese and ducks. Well before I reach them they start moving to the more inaccessible parts of the ponds. It surprises me, that in pitch darkness some of them take off and land on the water. Obviously they can see well in the dark. IR sensitivity, I tell myself. I envy them, and jog in the dark until I am past, then turn on my flashlight.

One of the benefits of going out this early is that I get to listen to the owls that live in the woods to the east of the park. Their conversations are lively and gentle, and I wish I could understand. Maybe in my next lifetime. I continue to be surprised at how many geezers like me are out and walking at that time of the morning. There are almost always dogs taking their owners for time in the exercise pens at Carrie Blake Park, yes, in the dark. First I hear the murmur of their voices and then the dogs set up a howl. It punctuates the quietness and reminds me that I'm halfway done.

One of the benefits of jogging the park is the restroom. It's heated, and there is warm water in the sink. It doesn't work to try to pee using cold hands. I have become an equal opportunity pee'r. I never met a restroom that I didn't use. I plan my whole jog around restroom availability. I just love being old. The plumbing takes on a personality of it's own. It has to be cajoled, fingers must be warm and you must be patient, patient, patient, and suspicious. You must not trust the stream to be completely stopped even after it has stopped. That makes it necessary to wear dark sweat suits. They allow you to experience that warm feeling just after leaving the restroom, but no one will notice.

After the restroom it's just a short distance to the bench by the duck pond. It's a neat place to sit, even in the dark. It's fun to listen to the quiet quacks that the ducks make then. Mists rise off the pond, and there are splashes as inbound duck find their way to the water. The glow of a rising sun is enthusiastically received by the ducks, and they start feeding and playing chase, and, sometimes, mating. First the male and female swim in circles about each other, bobbing their heads up and down. It looks for all the world like he is asking, "do you want to?" and she is saying "yes, I want to," and he asks "are you sure?" and she says "you bet," and they keep bobbing heads until they believe each other. Then she stretches her neck forward, with her beak low to the water, and he climbs on her back and grabs her by the back of the neck, and in 1.2 seconds it's done, the male leaves the back of the female, and swims in a fast tight circle around her with his neck stretched out and his beak cutting the water, signaling for all the other ducks to see that the deed has been done successfully. The female ducks her head under the water a few times to wash up, and it's over. Parts of that seem like human behavior, huh? It encourages me that someone is getting a little, and I head back towards the house.

I always jog so that I can see the oncoming cars. Some are very polite, and some not so much. I always get off the pavement, even when there is no sidewalk, to give the cars room. In turn, there are drivers that give me room. I like to wave a thank you, and when I do there is almost always a wave back and a smile. It confirms that I am part of a mostly friendly humanity.

Back home, I turn off my flashing lights, give my wife a hug, and cop a feel, and turn on the TV news. The news usually lowers my expectations for the day to a reasonable level, and I begin a whole new mostly unsullied day.

Not the end

Cause and Consequence

The grass looks greener there,
thought the gazelle.

That green grass ought to attract gazelles,
thought the cheetah.

The green grass and gazelles ought to bring cheetahs,
thought the hunter,
and he chambered a round.

The green grass, gazelles, and cheetahs brought hunters,
thought the lion,
as he licked his bullet wound
and then cleaned his claws
on a tree.

It Is So

It is so.
I have said it.
I have spoken words in the heat of argument
in alcohol smudged certainty
that I must be the rightest,
that loudness is some kind of substitute for truth,
that fierceness will make what might be true
and what is only guessed at,
into what is more right.
That unending repetition
is a valid basis for belief,
and if that isn't enough,
I will attach the words to music,
photographs, and humor
and drown out the personal thoughts of millions,
replacing their thoughts with my own.
I will become infallible,
in their minds,
and they will parrot my words
and the world will shout in unison
"Light beer is less filling."
Then the wise will laugh at themselves
and the silly will go home content
that they are in the majority.

A Dream

"Ahhh, to sleep, perchance to dream," I thought. Pretty Shakespearian for a mechanic, but definitely on target. Man, could I use some sleep. I have been on the road for four days, sleeping in the truck at rest stops, determined to keep my expenses down. Have you ever tried to sleep at a rest stop? Cars and eighteen-wheelers pull in and out all night. Weird dudes walk around at two in the morning, taking way too long a look at your truck. I'm cold, hungry, ran out of vanilla wafers two hours ago. Got half a root beer left, but it's flat.

Every once in a while, there's a lull, and it gets quiet. Then, I sense I'm about to fall to sleep. I've locked the doors 14 times, but I lock them again just to make sure, and roll the windows up so there's only about a ¼-inch opening, put on an extra jacket, and pull the cover up around my face. I can see my breath, but I'm fairly warm, and soon I drift off.

Sometime later, I don't know how long, there's a light tapping on the window, just beside my head. I'm groggy, but manage to open my eyes, but I close them again real fast, on account of I don't believe what I'm seeing. It's raining outside, and the drops have bubbled up on the window, and the moisture from my breath has caused the windows to fog up, well, everywhere except where my head had rested against the window. Only raindrops on the window between someone's face and mine. On the outside, there's a girl's face surrounded by the camouflaged hood of an old army jacket. In the darkness she looks like a ghost. It's a face like mine, I think, tired, on the road too long, the face of someone with not enough money to make ends meet. And she's wet. I roll down the window another ½-inch. By now I'm pretty much awake. "Sir," she said, "I've been trying to hitch a ride for the last two hours. I'm cold and wet. Could I sit inside your truck and warm up?"

I had heard about scams like this. They make up some excuse for you to let them in your car, then out comes a gun or a knife, and in a flash, you're watching someone else drive off in your truck. I looked the girl in the eye. I'm an experienced liar, and when you are one, you get to know the signs of a bald-faced lie pretty well. She wasn't lying. I let her in on the passenger side, then let her know that I was going to start the engine, just to warm up the truck cab. She nodded her head that she understood. Then she leaned her head back against the side of the cab and was out like a light. A pickup truck cab doesn't have a lot of room, so we were both trying to sit upright and sleep. It wasn't the most comfortable accommodation, but it sure beat the hell out of standing on the side of a highway in the rain. The cab warmed up quickly, and while it warmed I gave thought to whether I should drive on or not, but I knew that I was still too tired to drive. I found a rain jacket behind the seat and covered her with it, then I shut down the engine, leaned back against the window, and closed my eyes.

It was still very dark when next I woke. Damn diesel, winding it up tight, right there in the rest area. My second thought was, well I'm not very dead, so I must not have made a mistake in letting the girl in the truck. My third thought was, what girl? Sure enough, the seat beside me was empty, the seat was dry, the rain jacket was behind the seat where I normally kept it, and the passenger side door was locked. There wasn't even a teeny bit of evidence to show that there had been anyone there. Now, that got me wide awake. The rain had let up so I got out of the truck, walked around it twice, and seeing no puddle of oil and four tires still holding air, I rewarded myself with a trip to the rest room, a fresh bottle of root beer and a package of cheese crackers for breakfast.

Had I dreamed up the girl? If I did, I had a great imagination. Even hidden by the jacket hood, I had seen a face that was beautiful. Not cover girl beautiful, but beautiful like a flower or a sunset. I shook off the bewilderment, cranked up the truck, and headed out. By sunset tonight, I meant to be in Durango. My uncle there, had called me, saying he needed help, and asked me to come. My uncle was a mainstay in my life, took care of me when my hippy mom ran off with a preacher. Jeremiah Boogaloo, the pastor's name was. I hardly ever think good of him or Mom, but I always think good thoughts of my aunt and uncle. If he needed help, that's all I needed to know.

About 200 miles east of Durango, the truck needed gas, so I stopped and filled it up, then went inside to pay. I never keep my wallet in my back pants pocket, 'cause it cuts off the blood flow to the right leg after a while. I keep mine in my right jacket pocket. I reached in there, opened up the wallet, and paid the clerk. When I put the change back in the wallet, I noticed a slip of paper in there with the bills, I never put notes or anything like that in my wallet, and so it kind of piqued my curiosity. I stared at it over a cup of coffee for a while trying to make sense of it. "Call me," it said, and gave a phone number, a phone number with a Colorado area code. I didn't recognize the handwriting, and it sure as hell wasn't mine. It puzzled me, but I didn't have the time to ponder long. I hopped back in the pickup and soon Raton Pass was just a blur in my rear view mirror.

Turned out, my uncle needed help in taking care of his ranch. It wasn't a big one, about two sections worth, and 300 head, but he was getting on up in years. That wasn't all there was to it, though. I stayed there about a year. Every time I would get itchy feet, there would be another reason to stay. I took to wearing a Stetson, and in another year or two, I didn't want to leave. My uncle meant it that way all along. When he and my aunt passed on they left the place to me. It's comfortable, steady, and the neighbors are the kind you'd fight for. Life was good. Life is good.

Oh yeah, about that piece of paper in my wallet. I held onto that for about six months before I worked up enough gumption, and curiosity, to call it. Turns out the phone attached to that number, was located on a ranch about 20 miles west. I hadn't dreamed up the girl. Some things are just meant to be.

The Frog Just Sat There Staring

The frog was a large one, at least two pounds, sleek and slimy and, at the moment, "garunking" his heart out. The sun had set, the green water was warm, and the mosquitos had begun their hum and dance. Now, mosquitos are a good staple food source for frogs, and this frog had certainly eaten his share, as evidenced by the huge paunch hidden by his large folded legs. But this frog was looking for bigger and better things. The apple of his eye, the most difficult prize of all, was the beautiful metallic green dragon fly. They darted, they wheeled, they were grace and style, and...they were food. There was bound to be a spice to that green color that so enticed him. He interrupted his songs to send his deadly accurate tongue, now grown to a full six inches, to capture a nearby mosquito. "This night feels magical," he thought to himself. "Yes, there is something special about it."

The frog continued to sing. He sang of lost loves, of current loves, of loves not yet present. He sang of his grandfather, and his hero from frog elementary that had gone big time. That frog was now a professional jumper at the famous Calaveras County Frog Jump competition. And he sang of dragonflies.... "Garunk, garunk, garunk."

It was early in the evening. The moon was full, and made much light, and he suddenly became aware of a feeling that something was watching him! His great legs tensed, ready to propel him into deep waters. He was sitting in the shallows, and could feel no vibrations of a snake swimming, or worse, a heron, or a coyote walking through the water. He could hear no noises of approach. He could smell no raccoon. At first he could see nothing. The background noises of the crickets, and the other frogs were there, so they had detected nothing. He held still, scarcely breathing, waiting for a movement that would give away his adversary. But there was nothing, nothing until he realized that just behind him and to his right, sitting on a lily pad, was the most scrumptious dragonfly that this frog had ever seen.

"Why am I feeling alarmed?" he asked himself. "After all, this is food, and lots of it." That question faded as he became focused on getting within range of the dragonfly. He had never tried an over the shoulder shot with his tongue, but instinctively knew that he would have no accuracy doing it that way. He couldn't risk a miss. It would have to be a head on attempt. The frog stayed as still as long as he could stand the suspense, then, in tiny, tiny moves, he turned his body towards the lily pad, and the dragonfly. After what seemed like an eternity, he was lined up for a head-on shot, so now he just had to get within tongue range. There, just one more move, and that dragonfly would be nothing more than a full stomach, and a burp.

It would be a stretch, but the frog thought he could reach the shiny, green, delectable dragonfly. He tensed himself, getting ready to launch that tongue. But the launch never happened, for inside his head he heard the most beautiful sounds, more beautiful than the sounds of the night, more beautiful than a sunrise in the fog. It was the sound of a small voice, soft, melodic. The voice sang most sweetly, and the frog became lost in the beauty of it. When the singing stopped, he was disappointed, disappointed enough to croak "more."

The dragonfly turned to him and said, "You are too close. Please back away." The frog did as he was asked. "That's better," the dragonfly said, beginning to relax and flex its wings. "How is it I have never heard your voice before?" asked the frog. "We seldom speak," said the dragonfly. "But, your time draws near, and it is my task to tell you that you must prepare yourself." "For what?" asked the frog. "You have lived a full life," said the dragonfly, "and soon you will share yourself as food for another. It is the way of life, is it not?" "Yes," replied the frog. "I have been close to being a meal many times," he said. "I have always wondered what happens after that, or if anything happens."

"That is why I am here," said the dragonfly. "It has been the way of the dragonfly that we serve as messengers that go between this world and the next. You have three choices to consider. The first is to choose to exist no longer. When you leave life, your essence will become unfocused and will be absorbed by others. The second choice is to return to this life as a frog, living again from egg to tadpole, to frog form. The third choice is to choose another life form and to return to live that life. You must make your choice soon."

The frog considered what he had just heard for a moment, then said, "I have often admired the beauty of your kind, that you can fly, and visit the high places, and chase down mosquitos. I wish to return as a dragonfly." He sat silent, again, then asked, "can you give me proof that I might believe you?" The dragonfly was silent for a time, then answered. "The first proof is that I have spoken to you. The second proof is this." The beautiful sound began again, and then slowly, the dragonfly began to fade from the frog's view. Its wings shimmered, it's green metallic hardness softened, and it and the music faded.

The frog just sat there and stared in wonderment.............and then slowly became aware of the strong smell of raccoon.

In The Long Run

He looked up at the ceiling, listening to the sound of water in the urinal, and then closed his eyes and lost himself in thought. It had been a very tough day. He opened his eyes again upon hearing someone in the stall next to him, but stared straight ahead, the perfect example of bathroom decorum. After finishing, he flushed, zipped up, stepped back and turned to go, and froze dead in his tracks.

There standing in front of the urinal next to him, with eyes straight ahead, was a nine-foot tall green dragon! The man stood still, afraid to move. The dragon continued, oblivious to the plight of the man behind him. The man took notice of the dragon's green metallic scales, the small wisp of smoke curling from its nostrils, and its long tail that extended all the way across the bathroom and blocked his way out. He quietly backed away into a corner, trapped.

It seemed like the dragon pee'd forever. But now, it was about to happen. The dragon would turn, look at him and roar fiercely, its eyes glittering. It would take a deep breath and breathe out the flames that would incinerate him. In just a moment he would be a small pile of ashes heaped up on the blue tile floor. The dragon started to turn, and the man held his breath, quivered in fear, closed his eyes, and waited to die.

He heard the dragon move, he heard the claws on its feet click on the tiles, and he heard the metallic scales scrape the floor as he moved. But nothing happened. He opened his eyes in bewilderment. The dragon had turned away from him, had walked to the sink and was washing its metallic scaled forefeet. It reached over, activated the sensor on the paper towel dispenser, and tore off a paper towel. It meticulously dried its forefeet, and carefully disposed of the paper towel in the trashcan. It leaned down, looked into the mirror over the sink, and ran its claws through the scales on its head. Seemingly satisfied, it turned, leaned down and made its way out the door.

The man, still afraid to move, was acutely aware of the stench of sulfur in the room. After a few moments, he walked to the door, and very carefully opened it a crack, and looked down the hallway. The dragon was nowhere in sight. He opened the door wider, stuck his head out and looked the other direction. Still no dragon, no screams from the other parts of the building. He walked out of the restroom, his knees shaking, and sat down on the bench next to the water fountain.

A woman came down the hallway, and took note of the man setting on the bench, shaking and pale as a ghost. "Sir," she said, "are you OK? Do you need a doctor? I can call an ambulance and it'll be here in two minutes."

The man looked at her, shook his head no, and said that he would be all right in a moment. He started to speak, to tell her, "there was a...," and then he stopped himself. "Thank you very kindly for your concern, but I am feeling much better now," he said. Reassured, the woman walked on. "Perhaps," the man thought, "it will be much better in the long run, if I keep this to myself."

The man stood, paused for a moment, then walked slowly back to the oval office.

~

Choices

This all started with a stainless steel bolt. I needed a ½-inch bolt, 3½ inches long, and hardness 5 or better, to replace one that broke in my boat trailer. I knew that Hartnagle's Hardware had them, so I walked on over. I was in the process of crossing Race Street, when some weenie in a Dodge pickup truck came round the corner and ran over me. Killed me dead on the spot. Damned cell phone! It looked like he was trying to dial as he was coming round the corner. Man, the look that came over his face, when the front of the truck hit me! Well, that's the last thing I remember seeing, there was darkness, and then there was light.

It was kind of hazy at first, but bright, and I was able to see lots of others around me. Being raised Baptist, I expected all to be white tunics, white silk PJs or something like that, but it seemed that everybody was still in the clothing that they died in. Most were quiet at first, just standing there, looking around at the others, but eventually some began to talk, and then more. The questions seemed to be universal. "Any idea what's supposed to happen next? Where are we? Who's in charge? Where are we going?" ...stuff like that. Then the damnedest thing happened. There was a voice inside my head, a very calm and pleasant voice that requested that we please stay where we are, and said that someone would be there soon with answers.

I don't know if the others were seeing her as I saw her, but she was beautiful. She appeared in the midst of us, a group of several hundred. She was chastely dressed, but obviously the pinnacle of human appearance. After the crowd quieted, she spoke. "You are asked to reflect on your lives, and to decide whether you should go to heaven or hell." I looked around at the others, and saw some heads drop and sorrowful looks appear on faces. Others beamed, and others just weren't sure. The woman messenger faded from view, and a great murmur arose from the crowd.

We didn't have to wait long, ten minutes at best, before she reappeared. The voice in our heads told us to make our choice. "Those going to heaven, please go through the gateway on the left." That gateway was of ornately carved pure white marble, with metal gates made of what appeared to be gold. The gates opened to a cloudy path that led into a flawless blue sky. "Those bound for hell, please go through the gateway on the right." It was a terrible looking affair, and looked as if made of lava, all blacks and reds, crude, rough. The gate was one of those black cast iron jobs with spear points on each upright and barbed wire across the top, and it opened to an asphalt road that led down into fires and smoke, and dismalness of the worst degree. We could hear, off in the distance, cries of anguish and despair. "Please go now," she said, and again faded from view. Somehow, neither choice seemed right for me.

There was a general rush for heaven's gate, the sound of excited whispers, speculations about streets of gold, and the whereabouts of St. Peter. There was the reluctant shuffle of heavy feet, heavy hearts, among those headed for hell. There were some, apparently agonizing over the choice, that walked back and forth between gates. Eventually, even they made a choice. Finally, there were only three of us left. We stood there, and looked at each other, then at the others as they disappeared into the distance. As we watched, the gate to heaven closed softly but firmly, and then faded from view. The gate to hell was still open, but it was certainly not very inviting. There was this curious feeling though, that if I didn't hurry, I would somehow be left out. The others said that they felt the same way, but none of us could bring ourselves to enter, and eventually the gate to hell slowly, and with screeching hinges, swung closed. I felt a tremendous urge to run, to jump through the gate before it closed, but the three of us stood fast, watching, and listening to the tremendous clanging shut of the gates. A figure appeared on the other side of the gate, a figure traditionally devilish in appearance, with red skin-tight suit, black satin cape, jet-black swept back hair, and holding a three-pointed pitchfork. She stopped, looked at us in a most evil way and, with a gloved finger, tested the sharpness of the pitchfork. Then she winked, turned away and casually walked into the fires.

Hell's gate faded from view, and we were alone. And we waited....

***

We grew tired, and sat down on the cloud-like surface that we had been standing on, and began to talk among ourselves. One had died after cancer, the other from toxic poisoning from a new hair dye. I told my story of the cell phone death. Then we talked for hours about the lives we had lived. Still nothing occurred that gave us a clue as to what would happen next. We began to talk of food, of something to drink, and began to feel a tremendous frustration that nothing seemed to be happening.

As we sat, the conversation waned, and I thought about taking a nap. I put my hand down on what we had stood on, and found it to be firm, but with softness, a good place to lie down. Sleep would not come. I raised up on one elbow and again looked at the softness. I became curious and began experimenting. I reached out and pushed on the cloud and it offered some resistance. I waited a moment, then I stirred it round with a fingertip. To my surprise, the cloud began to swirl and an opening about two feet in diameter formed revealing an intense blueness beyond and, in the blueness, there were points of light. The other two souls watched, then did the same thing, and each experienced the same results.

"Ahhh," came a voice. "Your first acts of creation. You have made a choice, now, as the others made theirs. Yours is a path trod only by those who have reached spiritual and intellectual independence. Heaven and hell are journey's ends, choices made by those who view existence in more finite terms. Consciousnesses that make those choices have much to learn before taking the path you will follow. Come with me." And like kindergarten children, we took each other's hands and followed cautiously. As we followed the voice, the clouds around us began to clear. "You have lived lifetimes before," the voice said, "all with human appearances. Not all who make the choice you have can tolerate the change that it will make in your appearance. Let us see how you fare. Look at yourselves."

There were three softly glowing points of light where our bodies used to be. The voice spoke again and said, "Look upon me." There, where the voice seemed to come from, was another point of light. "This is the way," the voice said, "that we all began." For a moment we were all still, focused on the voice's light. "Try moving," it said. …and we did. At first slowly, in small awkward movements, then as we came to know these forms, we circled and chased, looking like fireflies on a hot summer evening. "Come," beckoned the voice. "Let those in heaven learn their lessons well, and those damned, too. We go now to have fun, to ponder the deepest questions of our existence, to evolve, to create. Follow me," the voice said, and four points of light streaked through an earthly summer night sky. The stars and planets glowed through the darkness in a friendly way, as we passed …and I felt, again, the exuberance of youth.

A Shoreline

I step off a Jamestown concrete walk
onto a sand path
winding through sea oats and grunch grass,
past the driftwood barrier
to where the water
tumbles sand and rocks about.
Gulls ride the winds
turning, soaring, ever on the alert
for a crab, a mussel shell delicacy
a fisherman's throw-aways,
a herring ball,
or French fries.
Clams squirt and duck under at my steps.
A Doberman runs about
ranging ahead of its human companion,
searching for a sniff of canine family,
of raccoons, coyotes, and foxes.
Sanderlings and pipers skitter,
cormorants skim wave tops.
Seaweed piles glow in morning sun,
with gossamer halos of sand fleas and gnats.
Damp wood, damp air, salty smell
shoreline in motion,
constantly unconstant,
peaceful, raging,
fun, or as solemn
as I need it to be.

I'll Never Forget

I had 36 cents, and cousin Benny had 40. It was a fortune for those times and in that place. Curve, Tennessee, was a small town of a few hundred souls, a farming community whose main interests were cotton and corn. The house that Aunt Gladys and Uncle Tolly lived in was a massive two-story with ten-foot ceilings, and it was located on a main road, Rural Route 2, that ran from Curve to Friendship, Tennessee.

Rural Route 2 ran past two churches, a small cluster of houses, and then T'd at the railroad tracks. At the "T," there was a rarely used railroad station and, across the street, a row of abandoned stores, their large windows empty, speaking of a time when cotton prices were better, and people had more to spend. Route 2 was a paved road, but the traffic was scarce.

Cousin Benny and I decided to take our money to the country store that was located down the hill about 200 yards, and see what we could afford to buy. Evenings were the best time to go there because Mr. Jennings would turn on the only TV for miles around, and people would come to see. We walked down the asphalt road, still warm from the day's sun, in our bare feet, taking note of frogs and tadpoles in the ditches, and sneaking peeks at Susie's house to see if she would happen to pass a window. Susie was the prettiest girl a pair of twelve-year-old boys could imagine.

Mr. Jennings' store was located where Route 2 and the road to the cotton gin came together. On this night there were more trucks and tractors parked outside than usual, so we knew the place would be hopping. Once you got past the gas pumps, there was a porch with benches on either side of the front. "Evenin," Mr. Jessup," we'd say. "Evenin, Mr. Simpson." "Evening, boys," would come the reply, and smiles, and then the men on the benches would go back to their discussions about wheel bearings on Ford tractors, and cotton prices, and about how Molly Jacobs was dating the Alford boy. We'd open the screen door and head inside the store.

The store had at its center a tall black coal-fired stove with small isinglass windows in the door, so you could see the fire when it was lit. Feed sacks were arranged in a square around the stove, about six sacks deep, just the right height to sit on and be comfortable. Besides providing a place to sit it provided the proper ambience in the form of smell. Feed sacks smelled of oats and earthiness. It smelled good.

On this night there was boxing on the TV. Joe Louis was fighting Rocky Marciano. The audience sitting on the feedsack seats and standing along the walls was equally divided as to who should win. We watched for a while, cheering with the others when a particularly good blow was struck, and then we started shopping, in earnest. Cousin Benny decided on an Orange Crush and Jujubes. I selected, after careful consideration, an RC Cola, and a Moon Pie. The soda was 25 cents, and the Moon Pie, a dime. We paid Mr. Jennings, and he gave us our pennies in change, which we carefully put away in our jeans pockets. "Thank you, Mr. Jennings," we said in unison. "Come again," smiled Mr. Jennings.

The fight was still going on and the place was packed. Even the bench sitters had come inside to see Joe Louis finish off his opponent. We went out front, and sat on those empty benches and listened to the fight, to the cheering and booing. We enjoyed, too, our treats and the clear skies, and the billion jillion stars. We heard the frogs singing along the creek. We listened to the 8:30 streamliner rumble past on its run to Memphis, and saw the lights and the passengers and the dining car flash past, and then once again to the excited folks watching the fight inside.

After a while, we started the walk back up the hill to cousin Benny's house. We were in no hurry, especially when going past Susie's house. Benny and I talked about everything during that walk back. About Uncle John in Korea, and whether he had had to shoot anybody, about school, and frogs and the best places to fish. We decided that we needed to go on a camping trip, and started planning that. It was all calm talk, fun talk, on a late summer evening that could not have been more perfect.

Benny went on to become a beloved high school teacher. He's gone now, but the memory of that evening is not. It brings me joy time and again. It's something I'll never want to forget.

The Pastor's Dilemma

His walk in the woods had taken him far. This was how he worked best. When there was need to work a particularly knotty problem, he would think on it, then put it out of his mind. Then he would walk through the woods until solutions would make their way into his thinking. It had always worked, until today. He was up to several miles distance, and still nothing was moving in that part of his mind. "I have to be patient," he said to himself. "I have to remember that not all moves at human time, that the universe has a clock that moves unencumbered, unhurried by the necessities of the human species."

And so it was that he found himself in an unfamiliar place, a place that had mists that rose in the trees, and smelled slightly of sulfur. There were small pools of water here and there, that he would put his fingers into and feel the warmth. It was fall, and the air was crisp. The huge leaves on vine maples were changing into their brilliant reds and oranges and yellows. The light movement of a breeze would bring a few floating down here and there, slowly spiraling to the ground in an ancient and elegant dance. A chipmunk sat on a the end of a fallen tree, stripping nuts from pine cones, quickly efficient, but vigilant, and at his approach, it scurried away under the fallen leaves, only to appear further away to scold the human for interrupting. He smiled and slowly moved on.

The man had not walked much farther when he noticed a quite large plume of steam rising through the trees off to his right. He decided to investigate. A well-used path led up a very steep climb that zigzagged back and forth up the hill. After about 15 minutes the path opened onto a pool larger than any of the others that he had seen, about 15 feet across the widest part, roughly oval in shape. Previous visitors had piled stones across the runoff of this hot spring to form a wonderful 1½ foot deep pool. The water was clear and hot, but not uncomfortable. Here and there around the edges there were logs placed to sit on, and there were remnants of candles, and flowers. He walked over and looked up the crevice that supplied the hot water and found an opening in the stone encircled by a black stain.

He looked back at the pool, and noticed off to his left, a fallen tree, whose branches were broken off. Those branch stubs formed a convenient place for hanging clothes. He looked back down the trail. He had seen no one during his walk here. Why not? He removed his clothes and neatly hung them on the branches, and winced as his bare feet found sharp stones as he climbed into the pool. The warmth was delicious, and his aching muscles were soon calmed. He laid back into the pool with only his face above the water, and looked up into a clear blue sky framed with green firs and brilliant maple leaves. All was quiet, and he drifted into a most restful and wonderful nap.

The man had no idea how long he had been asleep, when he was awakened by the raspy calls of stellar jays. They were large and brilliant blue with black heads, and black eyes that sparkled with mischief. There were five of them, and he was amazed at their precociousness, at how close to him they were. Something fell off to the side of the pool and the jays flocked to it. They made short work of it, but not before he noticed that it was a small piece of bread. The man realized, as his sleepiness wore off, that someone had to have thrown it. He turned his head in that direction and quickly covered his private parts when he saw the thrower. She was about his age, with sun streaked brunette hair, very attractive, and he knew her! She smiled and chuckled, and said,"you're too late pastor, I got a really good look at everything." The pastor was immobilized . There was absolutely nothing he could do, except make the situation more awkward. He waited silently, apprehensively, looking into her beautifully calm eyes.

"Pastor," she said, "when I have a really tough problem to solve I go for a walk in the woods, and always a solution comes to me. It appears to me that you and I solve difficult problems in much the same way. When my husband and I came to you last month for last resort marital counseling, I asked myself why I couldn't find someone like you, considerate, kind, and caring. I have since given up on Fred, and came here to figure out what to do next." She was quiet, then, and looked over at the jays, then threw the remnants of the bread to them.

She stood, dusting the breadcrumbs off her hands. Then, looking him straight in the eye, she said, "Pastor, I knew your wife back in high school. I know that she passed away four years ago. It has come to me that the universe works in some pretty powerful ways, that things happen as a part of some great plan that we don't know about and, when we ask it for solutions to problems, we sometimes don't understand the answers it gives." She walked away a few steps towards the trail, then turned back to me. "I'm not sure I understand the answer I've received this time..." She paused, looking again to the jays. Then she walked to the fallen tree where his clothes hung, and turned to face the pastor. Slowly, she began to unzip her coat. She looked the pastor in the eyes and spoke in a calm clear voice and said, "I'm not about to argue with the universe."

My Other Self

It's nearing the end of another long day at the wheel. Another water tower announces the name of the small town under it, another search for a one-night stay, whose major attributes are its low cost and clean sheets. A working TV would be nice but not necessary. I'll probably be asleep before my head hits the pillow. The clerk interrupts his impressive effort at controlling his boredom to check me in and I make it to the room barely in time.

I wake at ten AM, feeling fresh, and starving. A quick shave and shower, and I am out the door. Two buildings to the east there is a large parking lot with a rustic restaurant at the far end. I can smell bacon well before I get there.

"Jack," a feminine voice calls. That being my name, I turned around to see a real live cowgirl getting out of her pickup. Blonde hair, black Stetson, silver concho hatband, and jeans that showed off a knockout figure. That and a wonderful smile almost made me forget that I had no idea who this woman was. "Hi," I smile back. She walks right up and plants a very warm kiss on me, then looks deep into my eyes, holds my hand and says, "don't forget, we're meeting Jeanette and Charlie here at 7 for supper. Gotta run, hon. Gotta be at Doc Jenson's office, five minutes ago." She looks as good going away, as she did coming. She looks back, catches me staring and smiles again.

It takes me a full minute to find my tongue, and another 30 seconds to get it connected to my brain, and by then she is gone. When I am able to, I decide to go ahead and get breakfast, and do some heavy duty mulling over what just happened. It is an officially western restaurant, complete with a hitching post and fiberglass horse, and it is bustling. I open the screen door, and a waitress in a gingham dress comes towards me with a big smile and a large plate of bacon, eggs and all the trimmings. "Jack," she beams," saw you coming, brought your usual." She hustles me to a small table, puts the plate in front of me, gives me a big smile, and heads off to another table. When I finish, I leave her a large tip, but when she sees it, she picks it up and stuffs it in my shirt pocket, gives me a quick hug, and says "say hi to your momma for me." This woman let no grass grow. She is gone in a flash. No time for talk or questions.

Yes, yes, I am way curious. Two people seem to know me, in a town in the middle of Arizona that I have never been to. I walk slowly across the parking lot, hoping that the cowgirl will reappear, but no. Across the street there is a Rexall drug store. I need some razor blades, so I decide to go in. The store building is an old one. Just inside the door, on the left, there is a soda fountain behind a long white marble counter with twisted wire style stools. The ceiling is made with stamped metal decorations, and ceiling fans lazily turn overhead. The only person in the store is the pharmacist, and he is on the phone. He looks up and sees me, and says, "Hi Jack, I'll be right with you."

My curiosity is getting the better of me, and I am getting that feeling you get when everybody is in on the joke except you. Apparently, the druggist is having a hard time getting Miz Emma to understand why her medicine is making her dizzy. I find the razor blades and put them in front of the druggist. He rings them up, and makes change, and never skips a beat with Miz Emma. I leave the store still not knowing who these people think I am. I did check my wallet and sure enough, the driver's license verifies who I think I am and where I am from.

I sit myself on one of the benches on the porch. After about 10 minutes, I still can't make any sense out of what is happening, so I head back to the motel. I have the car packed in about 15 minutes, but I just can't bring myself to leave. I have to know. I head back to the drug store. There is a police car in front. I wonder what the excitement is. When I step inside, the druggist is sitting at one of the twisted wire tables. There is a policeman sitting at the table, just across from him, leaning back in his chair, comfortable, relaxed, his back to me. "Excuse me," I say. The druggist looks up, then sits straight up, looks hard, first at me, and then at the policeman. I look at the policeman, and there is something absolutely familiar about him. The druggist stands, then the policeman. Behind the soda fountain there is a mirror that runs the full length of the counter. "Look at this," says the druggist as he grabs me by the arm, and then the policeman. All three of us wind up looking at ourselves in the mirror.

The policeman looks exactly like me, and me like him. The druggist, the policeman and I are all silent for a moment. "You," I say to the policeman, "must be my other self, and I'll bet your name is Jack. " We all chuckle, sit and introduce ourselves, and talk the afternoon away.

I am invited to dinner, and there is a surprised cowgirl and waitress. Over time, I visited frequently, and eventually become a permanent and content resident, and to my delight, the best of friends with my other self.

Squeak and Homer

It is a cold winter night and it is quiet, unusually quiet, so quiet that Squeak, the mouse, awakes with a start. Squeak waits, curled up in his warm nest in the corner of the log cabin, trying to figure out what had awakened him. When nothing else happens, he gets up and sleepily goes to look outside the cabin. He pushes the drifted snow aside and peeks out. The moon is big and full and it is so bright that he is able to see easily. It is beautiful! The snow is smooth, the wind calm, and the stars sparkle like diamonds. There is nothing there, though, to awaken a mouse that was fast asleep. He takes a last look, yawns, and turns back to his nest.

Long ago, when the logs near the floor of the cabin had been fitted together, the man who built the cabin left a large gap between the logs. He filled the gap with mud and straw chinking to keep out the cold. One day last summer Squeak was around the outside of the cabin, hunting for something to eat, when he noticed that there was a hole between the logs in the chinking at the corner. Over the years the mud had cracked and a portion of the mud chinking had fallen out leaving a small hole, just the right size for a brave mouse to crawl into. For Squeak it was warm and deep and a great place to build a nest. It was not too far from his mom and dad's nest, so he could visit them and his brothers and sisters anytime. Squeak had carried in some dried grass and yarn he had found, made a nice snuggly warm bed, and climbed inside it. He was very happy in his new nest.

One day, a few weeks later, as Squeak snuggled in the deepest part of his nest, the chinking on the backside of the nest had moved and then had fallen out. When it grew light he went to check on it. He was surprised and very happy. Now, he could walk into the cabin without trying to go in through the front door. How marvelous a thing for the mouse! He could go inside or out as needed, without having to get past the cat. His grass bed pretty much blocked the cold air from coming in and the warm air from going out. He was a very happy mouse!

After looking at the snow outside, Squeak makes his way back to his nest, pausing to rearrange his nest of grass and wool yarn ends. Then he walks very quietly to the opening that leads into the cabin. There is a fire in the fireplace. The fire is low, and there is just the red glow of coals and an occasional pop or hiss from it. As he looks around the room, the fireplace pops loudly. "AHH," thinks the mouse, "maybe that is what woke me up." His question answered, Squeak decides that he is hungry. The mouse's eyes, quite good in the low light, see that the humans across the room are in their beds. His sharp ears hear the soft sounds of their breathing that tell him that they are asleep. "Now," Squeak thinks, "if I could just find out where that pesky cat is, then I won't get caught." Squeak looks and looks and looks, but he can't find the cat.

Squeak had not liked it when Homer the cat had come to live with the people. The mouse had to be constantly on guard whenever it went into the cabin. The food rewards were worth the risk, but there was a price. The mouse had a scar across his back, and was missing a piece of his tail, all caused by Homer. That is why Squeak is being so careful now.

After a few minutes of watching and waiting, Squeak decides that the cat must be up on the bed with the humans, in a place that he can't see. Homer often sleeps there. The smell of cookies is so strong that it makes him very hungry! Squeak's nose wiggles as he smells the cookies. Although Squeak stands on his hind legs, he still can't see the cookies that he knows are there. He hopes that the popping that woke him, had not awakened the cat. He wants Homer to be too sound asleep to hear him cross the floor.

The kitchen area is on the far side of the cabin, to the left of the fireplace. Squeak has to pass through the open area where the dining table is in order to get there. He scurries quietly from one concealment to another, from chair leg to table leg, till he reaches the table. Squeak climbs up the table leg, balances on the chair arm, walks quietly across to the table, and quickly finds the plate of cookies. He sinks his teeth into one and carefully climbs back down the table leg to the floor, where he sits and eats the cookie. His hunger satisfied,

Squeak takes a quick drink from Homer's milk dish, wipes his whiskers with his paws, and starts making his way back to his nest in the corner.

Squeak is very much afraid that the cat will catch him and eat him. He has seen it happen to other mice. With that in his thoughts, he runs quickly to the other table leg, then pauses, listening. No sound of Homer. Squeak runs quickly to the chair leg, and then... he never sees what is coming. Homer is up on the seat of a chair that had been pushed underneath the table. His sharp hearing catches the sound of the cookie being eaten and the sound awakens him, and just when Squeak is in the proper position below, Homer pounces.

Squeak knows that Homer has a good solid grip on him, and that there is no hope of getting away. He waits for the cat's game, where Homer will bite him, then toss him into the air, then catch him again as he tries to escape. Squeak wiggles and pushes, and bites Homer on his paw, but he just can't get away. He knows that he is firmly... and finally, caught.

Squeaks' heart beats very fast, his bright eyes are open very wide, and he looks up into the large golden eyes of the cat. The cat calmly returns the look of the mouse. There is something in the eyes of the cat that calms the mouse. It is not the look in the cat's eyes that he saw before, when he was almost caught. Squeak doesn't know what will happen next, but he relaxes, sure that he is about to be eaten.

After a while, the pressure of Homer's paws relaxes, and his sharp claws are pulled back inside. The paws are still in place, though, and Squeak does not move. He is still sure that he will soon be eaten. ...And then, Homer, still looking into Squeaks eyes, pulled his paws away, curling them underneath himself.

Squeak is very surprised by what Homer did, but is very careful not to move, not even a whisker. There is something in the cat's eyes, calmness, a kindness...something the cat wants him to know.

The mouse is very afraid, but he summons all his courage, and stands up. Still, Homer remains motionless. He does not get ready to jump on Squeak,

Squeak, after a few minutes does something no other mouse would ever do. He walks to the cat, and touches noses with Homer!

The cat sits for a little while longer, and then slowly and smoothly stands up and walks away!!!! He walks all the way over to the big rug in front of the fire.

Squeak is, again, so surprised that he doesn't know what to do. He waits to see what Homer will do. When Homer reaches the rug, he stops and turns, looking back at Squeak as if asking him to come to the rug, too. Squeak looks across the room to the corner where his nest is, and thinks about how warm and safe he would be if he were there now. The cat sees the mouse look towards his nest but does not move. Squeak surprises himself by walking to the rug, and then to Homer's side.

Homer lies down on the warm rug and then, after a little while, Squeak does too. ...and the two of them enjoy the warmth of a fire that feels as good as a mother's hug, and both doze off to sleep.

The cat was well fed. It did not need to eat the mouse. The mouse knew that the cat was in need of a friend. It did not need to run. Both decided not to do the things the humans expected them to.

After that night, each night when the humans had gone to sleep, the cat and mouse would meet by the fire. Homer knew that the humans considered it his job to keep mice away, and the mouse knew that too. Yet, both knew that good friends are very valuable, and they wanted to go on being good friends.

Homer and Squeak decided to make the humans think that Homer was doing his job. Homer would occasionally chase Squeak, so that the humans could see, catch him, and carry him out of the cabin, where they were sure the humans would think the mouse was eaten. What the humans would never know was that the cat would let the mouse go, unhurt, to be caught again later.

On the next day, the humans bring a small tree into the house and decorate it with shiny things and popcorn and cranberries on strings. They then put boxes beneath the tree, all wrapped in colored papers and ribbons. Next morning, the humans get up much earlier than usual, and build up the fire, and noisily open the boxes under the tree. The happy noises wake Homer and Squeak. Squeak is still for a while, and then he has an idea! Very carefully he sneaks over to the tree. The package wrappings that are strewn over the floor make that easy. The mouse finds his way underneath a piece of wadded up tissue paper, and then looks up towards the cat's favorite perch, in the chair seat under the table. Homer and Squeak make eye contact, and Homer knows what Squeak has in mind.

The humans are busy talking and laughing, but become quiet when they see that Homer is stalking something under the Christmas tree. When Homer pounces and "catches" Squeak and carries him outside, the humans are very happy. When Homer the cat comes back inside, he is stroked and fed tuna, his favorite food. That evening after the humans go to bed, Squeak comes out of his nest and into the house and finds, on the floor where the cat's bowl is kept, some bits of cheese and meat and milk left in the saucer. The mouse finishes his meal and makes his way to the rug in front of the fire where it joins Homer in enjoying the warmth of the fire.

And there is peace in the cabin, and there is goodwill on earth to mankind, mouse, and cat.

Boats and Captains

It is early.
The sun has not yet
found its way
above the edge of my world.
Its glow will find still waters
where orphaned boats wait patiently
for lines to be cast off
to be set free
to dance with the winds
to risk rocks and tides and shallows,
fair winds and foul.

We are, at once
boats and captains,
longing for still waters in a gale,
longing for enough wind to fill a sail,
wanting safe harbors,
wanting change that stays the same.
We are on a voyage through life whose secret must be
to enjoy the winds that find their way to our sails,
to shorten sail when the winds become bold,
to find joy in a raindrop,
peace in a fog,
beauty in rippled reflections,
clarity of thought
in still waters.

Incarnation

I am as a feather
loosed from a beating wing,
drifting through time
a cosmic breeze propelling me
from century to century
to come to earth
and become again
a part of the fabric of what is,
at that moment,
in that place.
It is a pattern as old
as existence,
as new as rebirth,
as constant as time itself.
It keeps our universe fed with
sparks of intellect,
new and revisited,
that are
its sustenance,
the engine that drives
our continued presence.

A Trip to Echo Lake

It is almost completely dark. The lake is placid, mirror smooth. The morning breeze is not yet stirring. The horizon is just beginning to show a tiny hint of the coming sun. Barely discernable in the lake, the black and white checkerboard pattern of a loon's feathers gives clue to its presence and its laughing call confirms it. A deer appears from the darkness, steps down into the water, and looks carefully around. There is grace in its movements, a lack of fear, and a presence of peace. It reaches into the water and drinks deeply, then raises it's head and is statue still. Only the water drops falling from it's muzzle disturb the water. Once again the loon calls, and is answered by echoes.

I am in my tent, snug in my sleeping bag. Only my face shows, and a cloud of steam from my breath. I look once more at the loon, then turn over on my back. I scoot forward just enough so that I can see the stars as they fade into a morning sky. The silhouette of a camp robber glides over me to land on the sitting log beside a barely smoldering fire. It hops here and there looking for supper's crumbs, and is joined by another. I turn back over to watch them and the fog hanging low over the cattails.

In the shadows I hear the bark of a fox and enjoy its echoes. Finally, I sit up and put on my hiking boots, no longer able to resist the crispness of the air and the mists. I find my canteen and make my way to the log beside the fire and reverently I sit. Martins find their way, scurrying along shore, making their low cooing sounds. Gradually, more birds awaken and their chatter makes the day more cheerful. An osprey folds its wings, dives, and reaches into the clear water to pull out a trout. It struggles with its load as it climbs to perch high in the top of a snag and have breakfast.

I am reminded that I, too, am hungry and open my pack to find trail mix and cheese, and I am content. The sun is now peaking over the horizon and I am warmed by a ray of brightness. I drowse.

I am reawakened by the plop of a lure in the water, launched by my partner's rod. She grins a good morning, her spirits undampened by the lack of bites.

And so it is that we start another day in paradise, glad for the weekend, glad for the trip to Echo Lake.

❧

Call It a Night

"I am so proud of you!" Dad said. "You are off to such a good start! You graduated from college last month and tomorrow, you start at a new job. Go ahead, have a seat, son. I'll get us something to drink. Iced tea, okay? We've talked before about jobs, about survival in the workplace. Well, I think that it's time to tell you more, like my dad did for me. I was in much the same circumstance as you, newly out of college, in my second week. I wanted to get to know my job quickly, to get comfortable with it, and to get rid of all those new guy fears; the fear of stuff you don't anticipate, the stuff you don't know, the stuff you were never taught, and the stuff that you have never experienced. Yeah, I know, you can never anticipate everything that you might need to know. I know that no matter how much research you do, there will always be the possibility of something unexpected, even when you're doing a task for the 100th time."

I again had the pleasure of spending a wonderful evening with Dad, learning from his experiences.

***

So there I was, excited at the new challenges, at getting to know new people, at the large paycheck, and afraid, all at the same time.

I was hard at it, and well into another ten-hour day, when a voice yelled from the end of the hall. "Hey, new guy, call it a night!"

"OK, Walter," I yelled, and shut down my equipment for the night. "Good night," I called out to him as I left. Walter was my supervisor. He had been with the company for 22 years, and had the reputation of being low key but highly productive. That combination of qualities had kept him in the good graces of his supervisors, but not in the line of those moving towards the throne of the company. He seemed to be content and comfortable where he was and, from what others told me, acutely aware of the politics of the organization. He must have been, they said, because he had survived three political purges in the last 10 years. He was great mentor material, and it was my plan to relate to him in that way, to ask his advice not on too frequent a basis, even when I had researched what seemed to be a perfectly solid answer.

***

My dad and I had talked many times about jobs, companies, and survival. He summed it all up in that last visit before graduation.

"Know your field technically, and that will help you get a job. Know your co-workers and supervisors, and that will help you do your job and to get ahead," he had said.

"Approximately two percent of the world's population is made up of assholes, with higher concentrations in some areas than others. Invest some effort in figuring out who the two percenters are, as that will help you keep your job."

"Evaluate your company as much as possible, and as quickly as possible, ...and if the concentration of full time assholes is greater than 10 percent, and the majority are in leadership positions, then it's time to start to look for another company, another job. You want to be somewhere where you will have good examples to follow and where good work is rewarded. Go find that place, mature and grow there. It will be a lot more fun that way. When you retire at the end of thirty years or so, you'll have a lot fewer mental messes to clean up and wind up with lot more happy memories."

"Plan on making mistakes and learning from them." Dad said that was a characteristic of most successful people.

"Lastly," he said, "you must know when to stop work, and start playing. Human bodies are the most sophisticated pieces of equipment you'll ever deal with. Maintain yours, don't abuse it, and it will be ready when you need it. You will have a family, eventually. Give them the time they deserve."

***

I was thinking about what Dad had said, on my way out of the building on my way to the parking lot. I remembered that the sky was clear and the stars were out. It was moderately cool out, so I put the top down on the convertible, and drove away. I drove about three miles and then found a place to stop along side the road. I pulled out my detector and walked around the car, doing my routine check for electronic bugging and tracking devices. I found one on the inside of the rear bumper, one in a pen in my briefcase, and one in the waistband of my pants. I put the pen in a metal foil bag, to block its transmissions. I then watched the stars for about 10 minutes. Then I did another check of everything with the detector. Sure enough, a backup had been switched on and, when it came on, I found it in my coat collar. I left that one alone, wanting the 2 percenters doing the bugging to feel moderately secure that all was well.

I thought to myself that Dad was right about going to this trouble. I drove on home and, after a change of clothes and another bug sweep, I rode my bicycle to Dad's house. There, over dinner, we worked out the subtle word traps to use in helping identifying those doing the bugging or those with access to the bug reports.

I was glad that Dad was retired and had time to work on this covert stuff. Someone in the company was tracking my movements, listening to my conversations.

I made every effort to bore the buggers to death. I was Mr. Straight Arrow anytime I was wearing my set of bugs. I gave them nothing that could be used as leverage. I planted weaknesses, and waited to see who would try to exploit them. I regularly fed identifiers to the buggers and came to know who was doing the bugging and, over time, came to know who in the offices I visited, was bugged. Then it came time for Dad and me to do a little bugging of our own. Dad used to say that being involved in this beat the hell out of watching TV and turning your brains to Jello. Dad said that he wanted me to have enough evidence collected on each bugger, before he died, that they could be brought to their knees, quietly, quickly, covertly, and at just the right time.

It's career building, all career building, Dad said. He often reminded me of how sick a society we live in, that does this kind of things to its members. Over time, Dad and I found that the asshole population of the company was just under 2% and that most of them were located in the front office. The company also met other criteria for my staying, such as having many good examples to follow, controlled growth, emphasis on product improvement and quality services, solid processes for keeping up with industry changes, and a solid history of living up to it's retirement promises. It looked like a solid bet for my future.

***

One day, years later, my supervisor, Walter, asked me to attend a meeting in his place. During the meeting, I had to take a pee break so I excused myself. As I made my way back to the conference room, I saw Walter at the conference room coat rack and, just as he was installing a bug, he saw me. I expected him to panic, but he just smiled, finished his work quickly, and then walked towards me. "Don't say anything to anyone about this," he said, "at least until we can talk. Come see me, right after the meeting, then you can tell whomever you feel that you need to."

My curiosity piqued, I returned to the meeting, and afterwards, went to Walter's office. He saw me coming, put on his coat and hat and met me outside his office door. I grabbed my hat and coat and joined him. He turned to Susie, our office manager, and told her that we were going to the Wickersham job site for the rest of the day. He told her that site was located down in a canyon where cell phones didn't work, so calls would not get through. He said, too, that we would be going home from there. As we left the building, he handed me a note. " I'm electronically bugged," it said. "Just follow my lead." He started talking about the job site and some difficulties encountered there, and about the staff meeting I had attended in his place.

He turned off the main highway, went through a residential area and into a park area. He parked in a place where we could see, but not be seen. He continued to talk about the job site, but reached under his front seat and retrieved, of all things, a bug detector, a Wilson Model 304a, the best in the business. He scanned his car, and me and identified the two bugs that I knew were on me, and two on him, and one on his car.

Walter and I came to know each other well, and because of that, we survived many a "2 percenter" inspired crap storm.

***

"It was comforting that my Dad was right about the way of things. I hope that you find that yours is too. Now take a look at this. It's Wilson Company's latest and greatest. It's capable of burst mode detection and decryption and can fry a "bug" from 10 feet away. It's my graduation gift to you."

The end and the beginning.

Dinner for One

The hawk's sharp eyes scanned the desert below for prey. Turning as he scanned, he felt the tug of an updraft from the cliff face below and turned sharply to find the greatest lift, and rode it upwards into a clear blue sky for at least two thousand feet. The flying was good and the hawk enjoyed the ride upwards, then resumed his scanning. He was in the mood for a fat prairie dog, but he had made a kill at the prairie dog town two days in a row, and now they were very skittish. There were other things below that were good to eat: ground squirrels, baby coyotes, snakes, and a favorite of his, lizards.

Lizards like to sun on the rocks in the morning sun, and in the evening just before sunset. This was a particularly hot day, so the hawk knew that even the lizards would not be on the rocks. He also knew that lizards, to find a relatively cool spot on really hot days, would climb the giant saguaro cactus. There, on the shady side of the cactus, they would drape themselves across the neatly rowed spines, and sleep. The hawk was checking the shaded cactus for the lizards, but so far, no luck.

During a particularly steep turn the hawk was noticing a new saguaro bloom located near the top of one of the arms on the cactus. As he looked at the blossom, he took note that in the shade below the blossom, there was a lizard's tail sticking out, and part of a lizard's foot. "AHHH," he thought, "a snack before dark. Just the thing for a good night's sleep." He continued his circular turns but allowed himself to drift downwind of the cactus. A few turns more to lose a little altitude, and he would be at just the right time and place for a quick dive to the hiding lizard. "There's the lizard," the hawk thought, and folded his wings in close to his body for the dive. His head lowered and his speed built to his liking, and just before his talons hit the lizard he spread his wings to slow his dive. He wanted just enough impact to stun the lizard and make it easy to grab hold of it. Then, he would, with two flaps of his wings, make his way to the top of the saguaro, a fitting place for a good meal.

He folded his wings and, with an expert flip, the lizard was in his beak and quickly swallowed. He savored the taste of it, and then began to preen his ruffled feathers. When the rest were in order, he shook his head feathers into place. From his perch he looked down on the blossom below. Somehow he was grateful that the blossom had survived intact and that, even from his perch, he was able to smell the sweet scent of it. He was grateful too, for his view of the setting sun, and the red and yellow colors of the nearby cliff. His hunger answered, he looked on with only mild curiosity as coyote pups played below. As shadows deepened, he heard the barking of foxes and the cooing of doves. "Tomorrow, I must find water, but for now," he thought, "all is good, ...and enough." A crescent moon rose and spilled its silent golden light over the hawk and his neighbors.

He wiggled his body to push down between the cactus spines and make the cactus top more comfortable, and then he tucked his head under his wing, his eyelids closed...and he began to dream.

Rules For Socially Acceptable
General Purpose Lying, Version 3

(Sources: observation of behavior of those around me, on TV, in movies, and in the newspapers)

If there's no way for others to verify what you're saying, feel free to lie.

If the truth will hurt someone, it's good manners to lie instead.

If you can't tell whether you personally are lying or not, it's a good lie.

If you're negotiating a business deal or selling something, you're expected to lie.

It's okay to lie as long as it's done in a humorous way.

If you will never ever see the people you are talking to again, it's okay to lie to them.

If you tell the truth, you're giving your competition an unfair advantage.

It's okay to lie as long as you're prepared to say, "I'm sorry," if you get caught.

If you are hazy enough about issues when you talk, any conflicts are then a difference of opinion and not a lie.

If you tell a lie often enough and increase the volume when you tell it, people will generally believe your lie.

Simple lies are the best. They are the easiest to remember.

Your credibility is much improved if you are consistent in your lies.

If there is enough money involved, current business etiquette requires that enough lies be told to complete the transaction.

The average person passes at least 50% questionable information per day. It's okay to make up a statistic that will support your current lie, while you are telling it, like I'm doing now.

Wishful thinking is an absolutely valid substitute for actual fact, and not a lie because you think that it's the truth.

If you don't know the facts in any given situation, make something up. The facts you make up will most likely not be true, but they will be comforting. Humankind is very good at this, because they've been doing it for such a long time.

Institutionalized lies are the easiest to believe, i.e. governmental, political, religious, or military. If you don't have an institution in which to house your lie, then invent one, and give its literature and videos a classy logo, with the appearance of wealth and power.

If you're getting paid to do it, it's okay to lie.

(In any other circumstance, it's okay to tell the truth.)

Lie sampler:

Half-truth: "I read that book," which translates to "the book sat on my coffee table for a year."

Accidental truth: A lie that turns out to be true at a later date.

Comfort lie: "We're going to be out of town that week."

Barefaced lie: The kind of lie that you tell when the listener knows you're lying. "The dog ate my homework, legal brief, etc."

Slippery Lie: "Relax dear, the bear outside the cabin has gone away."

Convenience lie: "I already gave at the office."

Partial truth: "I am 39 years old."

White lie: "I love that dress" (shirt, suit, hat, ?, may be substituted)

Sexual lies: The lies you tell to calm the reasonable fears of a sexual partner. "I love you" or "it was good for me."

Hopeful lie: The lie you tell yourself in hopes that it will turn out to be true. "I can win this election."

Outright lie: A lie that you tell yourself knowing that it will never become the truth. "I can win this election."

Institutional lie: It's okay to kill someone if your government, religion, political group, or chess club asks you to do it.

Commercial lie: It's okay to send jobs to other countries.

Endless

The Dream

In my dream, I was in Victoria, British Columbia, walking down a busy street, approaching a sidewalk cafe. My wife, Samantha, and Zack, a friend of ours, sat at a table, along with a woman I hadn't met before. When I reached the table there were hugs all around, and the woman stood and gave me a warm hug as well. We all sat down at the table and a waitress came and took our orders. Samantha and Zack started up their conversation again. It was a good-natured teasing conversation about buying clothes. I kept waiting for either Samantha or Zack to introduce the other woman at the table, but their conversation was so funny and intense, that it wasn't possible to get a word in edgewise. Zack began to tease me about needing to get some new shirts and I teased him about the Hawaiian shirt that he was wearing unbuttoned with a Panama hat. Not Zack's usual style. Just as I was about to ask them to introduce the woman at the table, Samantha and Zack's conversation took off on a new tangent.

Zack sat across the table from Samantha, and I sat next to her, and across the table from the woman. She was beautiful in a quiet way and, when she laughed at Samantha and Zack's remarks, it was a delightful, relaxed laugh. During the course of the conversation, both Zack and Samantha would glance at the woman in a friendly manner and included her in the geniality that we all seemed to feel. The woman was of a medium build, well proportioned, dressed in a dress of white gauzy fabric that came up to her neck and covered her shoulders, and was secured around her waist with a white belt. Her hair was white and her eyes were blue, and sparkled when there was laughter involved. Her teeth were white and even and she was altogether a handsome woman. I felt a reasonable amount of attraction to her, but not enough that it interfered with the comfort level of her being a part of the group.

We were most of the way through our meal when an unusual thing happened. I am a quick eater and had finished ahead of the others. The waitress removed my place setting and I rested both hands on the table in front of me. The woman finished up next and the waitress removed her dishes. The woman rested her hands on the table and, for a while, listened to Zack and Samantha. Then she turned to me and, leaning forward, she reached across the table and put her hands on top of mine. I immediately looked to Samantha, but she seemed not at all bothered by the hands. The woman's touch was warm and soft and she caressed my hands gently with her thumbs. I thought, "Whoa, this woman knows she's in front of Samantha and is still doing this. I've got to do something." Before I could, the woman stood, then Zack stood and gave the woman a hug, and Samantha reached across the table and gave her a handshake. Samantha and Zack sat back down and started talking again. The woman walked around the end of the table to where my left hand gripped the tabletop, as I prepared to get up to give the woman a farewell hug. She stopped and leaned her hip against my hand. I could feel the warmth of her through her dress. Again, I was concerned about Samantha being uncomfortable with what the woman was doing.

A look at Samantha revealed that she had noticed what the woman had done, but was not upset by it. The woman looked down at me, with a modest smile, then she leaned away, took my hand in hers and gently pulled me to a standing position.... and then led me away. I took a few steps then stopped. Samantha and Zack looked up. Zack smiled and waved. Samantha smiled and blew me a kiss. I was flabbergasted and hesitated, but the woman gently tugged at my hand. I blew a kiss back at Samantha, waved to Zack and overcome by curiosity, I followed her.

She walked purposefully, although she occasionally stopped to look in a shop window. She took a route along the seawall at the harbor in front of the Empress Hotel, then along a side of the Government building, then over one block to Beacon Hill Park. We walked at a slower pace through the park, enjoying the kids on their bicycles, the variety of birds, and the couples with infants. We turned off the main trail and climbed to the top of a low knoll and sat on a bench there. All sorts of things were going through my mind. I kept thinking sexual things, but there was nothing overt that encouraged that. We had not talked during the walk, but I was more comfortable with that than with anything I was thinking of to say, so I said nothing.

An offshore wind was blowing gently and there were a few wisps of fog that made their way in our direction, eventually enveloping both the hilltop and the two of us. The woman stood and, taking my hand, again pulled me to my feet. She hugged me, then took a step, still holding my hand. She looked at me with the gentlest of smiles, her blue eyes blazing laser bright. "Come with me," she said, and then almost shyly she added, "I am death." Had it not been for the touch of her hand on mine, I would have run. I felt no fear because of that touching and followed her into the mist.

Of Mice and Men

In the forests far to the south of town there is a meadow. There, down in the earth, about two feet below the surface, a small brown mouse begins to stir. As it awakens, the mouse's first order of business is to check the smell of the burrow to see if it is normal. It is midsummer. The earth is warm and damp, and the rich smell of humus fills the burrow. There is no smell of weasel or coyote, fox, cat, or snake.

Mice like to sleep during the day. When darkness starts to fall, they make their way through their burrow to the main entrance and then the secondary entrance, to make sure that they are both clear. Cows, deer, horses, and those dratted humans are good at collapsing a perfectly good entrance and making more work for the mouse.

Both are open today. Next, it's out the main entrance to see what predators are around.

The main entrance to mouse's burrow opens out under the roots of a large bush growing on the side of a shallow gulley that runs through the meadow. It's funnel shaped so that when the mouse is running at top speed, he can dive into the opening more easily and have inertia force him inside the burrow. That split second saved has rescued him time and again from an all too close predator. Once inside the opening, the burrow curves gently up and in for several feet and then opens up into a sleeping chamber lined with soft warm grasses. The burrow continues on up past the sleeping chamber to just below the surface of the ground so that if a predator starts digging into one of the entrances to the burrow, the mouse can quickly finish digging to escape outside.

When it's time to go outside, the mouse climbs the bush outside his door so that he can see better, and further. Before night falls, he scans and sniffs for close-in predators first, then checks the nearby trees for hawks and owls. For now, there are none and so he begins a search for his favorite leaves, insects, nuts, seeds and berries. In short order, the mouse is full and climbs a bush to a resting spot, also a fine viewpoint. He is alarmed to smell smoke and, in the dimming evening light, to see the glow of fire. His instincts tell the mouse to run for his burrow, but his intelligence tells him that the fire is small, and not growing. The mouse can see the shadows of men moving about and hear their voices and sense the heaviness of their steps. He can also smell their foods, which are unfamiliar but interesting. He decides to move closer and see what the foods are.

There are many creatures that can see well in the dark, so the mouse knows that he must move carefully, always on the alert for the sound, motion or smell of a predator. He runs from one clump of grass to another, through tunnels in the grasses made during past foraging trips. He checks for dogs and cats, as he grows closer to the campfire. There are horses, which he prefers to keep out from under, so he makes his way around them and follows his nose to the saddle-bags where the food is kept. The mouse can't approach the saddlebags right away, because the humans are still awake and moving around. He decides that it would be best to find a high viewpoint and wait till the time is right.

Several hours later, as the fire dies down, the humans find their way to their sleeping bags. Soon, there are snores, snores that drown out any sound that a mouse might make. When no human moves for a while, the mouse makes his way to the saddlebags and enjoys the edibles there. When he has eaten all he can, he begins to explore other saddlebags and finds something warm that will make good nesting material. It is long but he is able to drag it fairly easily because it is not wide. After a minor struggle, he is able to drag the item from the saddlebag, unrolling it as he moves along. The mouse stops at the edge of the closure flap of the saddlebag and looks out to check for predators before leaving the protection of the bag.

The fire dies down to coals. It gives plenty of light, but the mouse's normally superb night vision is being partially obscured by it. The smell of the horses and humans is strong and interferes with detection of other predators. The snoring of the humans is not only an annoyance, it covers any sound that a predator further away might make. This is going to be risky, he thinks. The mouse drags the cloth out of the bag and starts on his way towards his burrow. As he leaves the light made by the coals, his movement catches the eye of an owl perched high in a nearby tree.

The owl is patient, watching the mouse working hard to drag something through the bushes and grasses. The owl knows this mouse and his burrow, and has come close to catching him on more than one occasion. Perhaps tonight fortune will smile on the owl. The owl knows that he has to wait until the mouse gets close to his burrow to swoop down on it. Mice tend to eat the vegetation away in a radius of about ten feet of their burrows, making it almost clear of obstacles to the owl's flight. And so, it watched, and waited, it's anticipation growing. The mouse was growing tired of pulling its burden, but he has not survived this long by being careless. He stops frequently, sniffing, listening, looking. Once he ducks back into a grass tunnel, when the scent of a coyote is noticed. The mouse knows that the coyote had passed some time ago, so he proceeds on. The mouse has to pee, but he knows that if he does, every sharp-nosed coyote within a 50-foot radius will know where he is.

The mouse is getting close to the burrow entrance now and becoming more and more exposed to attack by the owl. The owl senses that the time is right, spreads his wings and launches silently into flight. Slowly at first, then faster and faster he flies. Reaching out with its talons, he can almost taste the mouse even now. The mouse senses it coming, and scrambles under the cloth he had been pulling. The owl sees what the mouse is doing, and when he strikes, the owl seizes the cloth, hoping to catch the mouse as well, then flaps his wings to climb to a perch. Something is wrong. What the owl has in his talons does not feel like a mouse. It does not struggle as a mouse would struggle, nor squeak in terror as a mouse would. Then the owl feels whatever it has in its talons catch in the bush over the burrow entrance.

The owl struggles with his burden, beating his wings mightily for a moment, then lets go, and flies away. The mouse lets go of the cloth and drops to the ground. He cannot believe his good fortune, and dives into his burrow. His heart beats wildly and he is breathing hard. He makes his way slowly to his sleeping chamber, where he lies down with a groan, and rests.

***

The next morning, just after sunrise, the horsemen break camp, all the while complaining about a mouse that had gotten into their food. The four men mount up and start across the meadow. They only go about 20 yards when one of the riders halts his horse and dismounts. "What the hell are you doing, Red?" called one of the others. Red walks to a bush and pulls something off the top of it and turns to the other riders. "I'll be damned," he says. "This is my sock. Nobody wears striped socks but me. I came up short one sock this morning when I put my clothes on. How the hell did it get here, he asked?" He turns the sock over and takes note of the tears in it where it had caught on the bush, and where it had been pulled on by the owl's talons. "Well, it's trash now," Red said. He sees the entrance to the mouse burrow and bends down on one knee, then stuffs the sock in it. "Maybe," he says, "the mouse will have a use for it." The other riders chuckle, Red remounts, and they go on their way.

***

"Damn," thinks the mouse, "something has stopped up my main entrance." He makes his way up to the blockage and begins to dig. He quickly discovers that the blockage is the very cloth that he had dragged back from the campsite. He scratches his head for a moment trying to understand how this could be, then goes back to digging out the cloth and dragging it back to his sleeping chamber. This winter he would be warm. "At least," he thinks as he works, "this time I'm not digging out through cow dung."

Dear Tony

Thank you so much for bringing your family to share my 70th. What a delightful visit!

You asked during that visit, if living 70 years had produced any insights or wisdom. I had to think about that for a bit. It's a valid question, and deserved a better answer than I gave. I'm not so sure that what follows is wisdom, but these concepts seemed to work for me. Living this long, surviving this long, probably doesn't happen by accident. So, here goes:

1. Don't expect things to stay the same. What you have in common with those around you is that you are experiencing a similar rate of change. That can become different in a heartbeat. Enjoy your family, your work, and your life now. Don't plan on there being a later.
2. You're on the right track if you catch yourself doing more things that you like on a daily basis, and doing less of the things you don't care for. Don't mistake tolerance for liking.
3. Beware of those who deal in absolutes, those who expect every outcome to be 100% of what was wanted, what was expected. Work for a high percentage but don't frustrate yourself and those around you by expecting too much. The cost of any effort increases exponentially after you reach 95% of expectations, in terms of stress, and expense.
4. Think only enough about the future to establish a tentative plan on how to get where you think you're going, and only enough about the past to learn the lessons provided by past mistakes. Allow the bulk of your mentality to be spent on what is.
5. Expect to make mistakes. They can be one of the best learning tools around. Keep in mind, though, that you have to survive the consequences to learn anything.
6. Every once in a while, participate in someone else's reality. It's best when it involves someone that is a relative stranger to you. It usually gives you an opportunity to assess how sane you are.

7. Don't expect anyone's concept of reality to be the same as yours. Be tolerant of the realities of others. Beware of cultural shape shifters that build who they are out of bits and pieces of other's realities, with no valid reality of their own. Trying to figure out how to deal with them is pretty much a waste of time.

8. Be careful of who you choose to follow. Choose someone who knows how to appreciate you and your talents, who helps you grow personally and professionally. Don't expect them to be correct or right 100% of the time. When they are wrong they need to know, but don't expect them to always react in a positive way, even if you deliver the information in a most courteous way. If they are self destructive, keep your distance. You don't want to go down with the ship.

9. Give trust only to those who earn it. Even those you trust the most will occasionally foul up. Don't expect to be able to trust anyone 100% of the time.

10 Find another home for the stuff in your life that you don't use. What you don't use or enjoy will become a burden, whether it's old clothes, or memories.

11. Everything that you call yours comes with a need for maintenance. Only keep what you can afford to maintain, in terms of time, energy, and money.

12. Care for your body and mind. Be careful with what you put in them. Make sure that both are provided with enough exercise and rest.

13. Don't take life or humanity too seriously. Associate as much as possible with those who seem to be able to balance work, play, and family, and to have fun being involved in all three.

14. The best decisions are made when more logic and less emotion is involved. Be suspicious if someone is attempting to influence your decision by using emotion. It means there is probably not enough logic available to support their position.

15. What people say and what they mean is not always the same. Try to understand what they mean in spite of what they are saying.

These ideas have been tested by time and trial, and adjusted over time to what you see here. I expect them to eventually change. Please keep in mind that I trust them about 95% of the time, and that I wasn't able to follow my own advice all the time. :-)

I hope that you find something of value here.

Happy New Year, and best wishes to you, Jilda, Aileen, and Reanne.

Love,
Uncle Terry

The Opera Box

There was elegance
from doorway
to stage.
Highly polished brass to crystal chandelier,
from mahogany, rich with polish
to carpet and burgundy velvet curtains,
immaculate.

Elegance was reflected
in clothing,
formal, black, carefully pressed.
Shoes shined,
freshly trimmed hair combed to perfection,
shaved, washed, and scented,
carefully chosen jewelry providing sparkle.

In dresses of satin and lace,
tight bodices,
matched shoes,
handbags and wraps
in coifs by Renaldo, and
French perfumes.

To be sensed and seen,
to see
and then to hear,
that is the goal.

After carefully posing in the lobby,
making small and large talk
of singers, dancers, and watchers,
ladies take their gentlemens' arms
and make their way to their opera boxes.

Women carefully arrange dresses and smiles
on Louis XIV chairs,
Men take their seats
and look about,
taking their partners hands,
as the house lights dim,
once, twice, three times.
The murmur of voices in the audience fades
as the overture begins,
lights again dim,
heavy velvet curtains whisper open.
A spotlight slowly brightens
showing a delicate maiden
of significant girth
lying on a fiberglass cliff, darkness all around.
On her head, a horned Viking helmet.
A leather bodice struggles to hide
her tremendous cleavage.
From deep within that cleavage,
a mezzo-soprano sings mightily,
"Siegfried! Siegfried!"
and the opera has begun.

In Box 32 A,
I fidget in my rented tux,
absorbing culture,
wondering how a freckled boy from Tennessee
found his way to an opera haus in Wiesbaden.
My interest brightens when I notice
a quality in the voice of the singer,
a tone a lot like
my Aunt Ruby, calling us to supper,
and I smile,
and try to understand the German lyrics.
I glance to the opera box to my left

and a stunning lady catches my eye
and I hers.
and we blush in unison.

"Brunhilda," a deep baritone sings.
Ah, the hero has arrived.
They hug,
and in perfectly indecipherable German
subtly announce what is to come.
I hear the door to my opera box open and close,
and I look back.
I move over to make room.
Stunning lady now sits by my side, smiles,
and in a low voice, translates the actor's lines.
I am immersed in culture and refinement, and pheromones.
The opera box is quiet witness
to a wonderful beginning.

The Second Time Around

The mechanic at the service station said that he could get a new fuel pump delivered and installed in two hours. I asked where I could get a sandwich. He sent me to a drug store across the street and down two doors. The street was made of red brick and was wide for such a small town. I crossed it, marveling at the workmanship in it, that it had been in place for over a hundred years. Few things in civilized society last that well.

The sandwich was great! It was a BLT on dark rye, with a pickle slice, and French fries that were amazingly greaseless. The conversation with the waitress had even more sparkle than the soda she served. A cherry phosphate, she called it. In less than 30 minutes I was provided with an in-depth history of that small town in Arkansas, and a life story that amused with it's clever insights, and contentedness. Afterwards, I needed to stretch my legs and walk off the lunch, so I asked her where there might be things of interest to go see. She rattled off a few tourist things, then grew thoughtful, looking me over as she thought. "Terry," she said, (we had long since gotten to first names) "do you like antiques, old tools, arrowheads, stuff like that?"

"Jamie," I said, "I sure do."

"My sister runs a store like that, not far from here, in fact about six doors down on this side of the street, out the door and to the right. It's called The Second Time Around. Her name is Jessie."

I left her a generous tip and slowly made my way down the street, taking in the sights and sounds. All the storefronts were brick, nicely painted and trimmed, tidy looking places with swept sidewalks, and potted flowers. The clothing was pretty much the same for all, jeans, t-shirts, and ball caps being the order of the day. I had finished lunch after 1:30, and in this town, on this hot August afternoon, the pace seemed to slow perceptibly. Probably, I thought, my fuel pump is going to take longer than the two hours estimated.

A voice, soft and southern, spoke my name. "Terry, that you?" she asked, a twinkle in her eye?

"That's me," I said, bluffing past the shock, and smiling back. "You must be Jessie," I said. "Jamie called you?" I asked.

"Yes," she said. "Come on in, it's way too hot to be outside." She held the door open for me, and as I passed, the subtle fragrance of her was a pleasant thing, a reminder of other beautiful things, flowers, and the like. She was my age, maybe a bit younger, not skinny but well proportioned, well built, just like (I was to find out) her personality. She wasn't the magazine cover kind of beautiful. Hers was the effortless beauty that showed more from being with her than from just seeing her. There was this lingering sense that I knew her vaguely. But no, that was highly unlikely, as I had never been in this state before.

The inside of her store was like the front, well cared for, uncomplicated, but laid out in a fashion that teased the imagination. Jessie said that Jamie mentioned that I collected, or had an interest in old photographs, things Indian, and in old tools.

I expected her to point me in the direction to go, but she stayed with me, and we shared a delightful hour or so. I found two great flint arrowheads and a brass civil war uniform button, and purchased them. She wrapped them carefully and put them in a box, then with a caution that she would be right back, she hurried off through a door marked private. I thought on the short time I had spent here and how I could not shake the feeling that I had known this woman before. She came back shortly through the door with a smile, and a small ribbon and tissue wrapped rectangle about 4 x 5 inches in size. "Now Terry," she said, "I have something extra for you, but you must promise, that you will not open it until you are at least 200 hundred miles from here." I promised.

I was surprised, grateful and gave her heartfelt thank you's. I shook her hand, and breathed in her fragrance deeply, but discretely, and said goodbye. She didn't say goodbye, but said she hoped our paths would cross again. The twinkle was in her eye. If only I wasn't in such a hurry...(damned conference).

By this time I knew that the mechanic's name was Alford, so when I walked into the garage I called out, "Hi, Alford, is the Ford ready?"

"Sure enough, Terry," he said. "I was just finishing up the bill." Jamie and Jessie were right about Alford. His pricing was right and the Ford ran great. "Y'all come back now," he said. He waved as I drove out of the garage, and Jessie waved from across the street.

It was getting late in the day and I had to finish the drive to New Orleans by that evening. I had a presentation to give the next morning, so I yielded to the pressure to practice it as I drove. By the time I reached New Orleans, I was exhausted, so I went immediately to bed. The next morning, I gave as sparkling a presentation as the subject would allow, and was rewarded with approving comments, and asked many questions. At lunch I met with George, my headquarters counterpart, and a person who shared my great interest in Indian things and photographs. George was an expert in early photography, daguerreotypes, tintypes, that kind of thing. I mentioned my purchases to George, who became very enthusiastic about seeing them.

I brought them down from my room, to George, who waited in the lobby. I told him in detail about the Arkansas town, and the people there. He was really envious of the flints and the uniform button, but became very curious about the ribbon wrapped package, and asked if I would open it. It was a photograph, a daguerreotype, and George immediately snatched it from my hands, carefully holding it to prevent fingerprints.

"Terry, this is extraordinary," he said. I could see over his shoulder that it was a photograph of three people dressed in clothing of the civil war period, behind a hitching rail, complete with horses, in front of a brick store. "This is an authentic daguerreotype, taken by one of Matthew Brady's assistants," George said. "I recognize the name of the photographer on the back of the photograph. The date on the back is May 10, 1864, and from the material that the print is on, and its appearance, I would say you got yourself a great find!" He was as excited as a school kid finding a fifty-dollar bill. He pulled out his reading glasses, and began to look very closely at the photograph. He stopped his cheerful chatter, and became very quiet, then slowly looked around at me.

"You'd better take a look at this," he said. The first thing I noticed was the brick street, then the storefront. It was the town in Arkansas, the town where I had the car repaired. The storefront was Jessie's secondhand store. Then I noticed the three people in the photograph. There was a small boy, standing with what must have been his mother and father. I looked more closely, and even though the figures in the photograph were small, their features were recognizable beyond any doubt. The woman was Jessie or an absolute look-a-like. But that could not have been what George saw that turned him serious. He didn't know Jessie or the town. I looked at the man in the photograph. It was a picture of me.

"How did you do this?" George asked. "Photoshop?"

"No, George," I said, in a tone of voice that told him I was both deeply affected by what I saw, and was telling the truth.

"It would seem that you have somewhere you need to be," said George. "Call me," he said.

I had two weeks of leave saved up, so I called my supervisor and arranged to go on leave.

***

The door to the storefront was open when I drove up. "Welcome back, Terry, " Alford yelled from the garage. I waved back at him, and turned to find Jessie smiling at me from the doorway.

"Come on in," she said, holding out her hand. "We have a lot of catching up to do."

My Valentine

I worked on it for two whole hours. Cutting, pasting, writing, rewriting, getting it just right, saying stuff that would make her feel special, without being mushy.

She was in my third grade class. She sat in the third row back from the teacher, in the second row from the classroom door, and was in the row one seat ahead of me and to the side. It was kind of neat, because I could take a peek at her every once in a while, and not get caught by her, or by the teacher.

I first noticed her when she answered a question the teacher, Mrs. Johnson, asked about geography. There was something about her voice, something smart and calm and knowing, and kind of grown up. She wasn't a "smarty pants" that stuck her hand up at every question, but she answered questions several times in a day.

I began to notice how she dressed, and how her hair smelled like peaches, and how she hummed to herself as she did math problems. Sometimes I would ask her for help even when I knew the answer, just to see her eyes and her smile.

Sometimes I would see her at recess, playing with Marjorie and Jennifer. She was strong and quick, and could throw a ball well. I liked it when she did jump rope, and her long hair would fly in the air and the sun would shine through it.

I liked to climb on the monkey bars with my friends, Mark and Jake, and to play catch, and talk about baseball cards. Whatever I was doing, I would make sure that I could be in a place where I could see her every once in a while.

I decided to make her a Valentine's card, and that she would be my secret valentine. That way the guys wouldn't find out and kid me about her, like some guys did to Charley, who sits behind me. They didn't need to know that I liked her.

The day came in class when everyone was supposed to bring in valentines and leave them on the desks of whoever was to get them. I didn't give anyone a valentine last year. None of the guys gave cards to other guys. It was mostly girls giving cards to girls.

I went to class early, before anyone else got there, and left the card at her desk. Then I went back out to my locker in the hall to leave my backpack there. She would be without a clue as to who the valentine came from. Mark came while I was at my locker and asked if I had done my homework. He said that he had a hard time with it, so we looked at the math problems, and I helped him with the addition. It was the carrying over part that he was having a hard time with.

Then the bell rang. It was hard, but I kept myself from looking at her as I walked to my desk. I sat down and the teacher took roll, and after my name was called, I looked down at my desktop and there, under the homework I left earlier, just barely sticking out, was the edge of a valentine. After the teacher finished calling roll, she announced that we would start our celebration of Valentine's Day by opening valentines, and then we would go through our math homework.

I was really curious about who had sent me a valentine, so I opened it up quickly. It was from a secret valentine. That really got my curiosity up. I looked around the room, but everybody was busy reading their cards. I picked up the card and kind of tapped the end of my nose with it and, when I did, I noticed it, the faint smell of peaches. I looked up at her just in time to see her look at me and then turn towards the teacher. She didn't turn in time to hide the smile that was on her face. I was pretty sure she saw my smile, too. I kept on smiling for a while after that. I wasn't sure what I was feeling, but it sure felt good.

Barbed Wire and Band-Aids

They were small cuts. Three in a row spaced about three inches apart, and about a half inch long. Fortunately, they weren't deep. Two Band-Aids covered them just fine, and nobody knew how I got them but Bruner, and me.

I live in the south central part of Montana, in a small town called Denton, at the corner of Bower and Main. It's a small house, not too far from the high school, nor from my friend Bruner's house. Bruner and I will be seniors this fall. Summer in Denton is hot and dry, and the terrain here tremendously, overpoweringly flat. It is boring, boring, boring. Bruner and I needed something to do, something unusual, something wild.

We were sitting outside the Dairy Queen, on a Tuesday night, when the 10 PM train came rumbling through. In a stroke of brilliance, we decided that train needed someone to ride in one of those boxcars all the way to Nancy's house. She lives about three miles west of town. The trains slow when they pass through town, so we walked the half block to the tracks, turned where the tracks ran past Eldridge's Hardware, and there we each grabbed the bar on the rail car next to the sliding door and swung aboard. The boxcar was empty, and the doors on both sides were open. We watched what little there was of town roll by, and heard the clanging of the bell on Banks Street crossing. It was dark so no one could see us. It was like we were pulling off this big adventure. We did a lot of grinning.

There was a train trestle that crossed the river, marking where we would have to get off. Then we would walk north through the woods along the river, and under the Highway 81 Bridge. A quarter of a mile, and we would be within peeking distance of Nancy's house. The train was still moving fairly slow, as it had a fairly sharp curve in the track to negotiate in another half mile. It was easy to swing off the train, and we both managed it without getting banged up.

Our destination was a two-story house that sat on the high side of the river where it crossed under the highway. It was a pleasant house. Nancy's family kept it looking good. The main thing that we liked about Nancy's house was Nancy. She was a great looking girl with lots of curves, and a great sense of humor.

The hardest part of the walk was staying on the cow trails. We had a quarter moon, so that gave us some light. Our plan was to get up close enough to the house to catch a peek of Nancy's curves, as she got ready for bed. What we didn't count on was Nancy. She liked to sit on the porch after sundown, look over the river, and listen to the night sounds of the herons and frogs. We had to climb through a barbed wire fence to get to Nancy's house, and when we did, we disturbed some of the cows that were lying there. They just got up, and moved off a ways. No noise, no ruckus, so we figured we were OK. Except For Nancy, we would have sneaked in without anyone knowing. Nancy knew her cows and their habits. She knew that once down for the night, that they wouldn't move unless something disturbed them. Nancy kept a pair of binoculars on the front porch, for watching birds and things, and she used them to catch a glimpse of us heading up to her house. It didn't take much for her catch on to what we were up to, and apparently less time to figure out how to have some fun.

She went and got her dad and mom, and let them in on what she was about to do. Dad grinned, said he knew a way to liven things up a bit too, and got his shotgun. He went outside to where he knew the boys would have to go to see in Nancy's upstairs window and hid. Mom went in the kitchen and made noise washing dishes to distract the boys from seeing Nancy's dad. Nancy went upstairs and turned on the lamp in her bedroom.

The boys saw her light go on, and were beside themselves with their good luck. They grinned and went even faster so as to get there in time for the big show. There was a shed where the tractor was parked. The boys figured that they would lessen their chance of getting spotted if they went to the far side of the shed and kept it between them and the house. Nancy's dad figured the same way. He was inside the shed, and had a window opened next to where they would peek around the corner.

The boys were stealthy as cats, except for an occasional muffled giggle. They looked at the kitchen window and heard Nancy's mom washing the dishes. Nancy moved randomly, tantalizingly back and forth across the upstairs window. Then she pulled down the window shade. Her silhouette showed on the shade perfectly. Then she began to take off her clothes. The boy's giggling stopped. For the boys, all sound stopped, and there was nothing else in the world except that shadow on the window shade.

Just about the time that the shadow on the window shade reached around to unhook her bra, Dad decided that the boys had seen enough. He pointed the shotgun out the window and up at the sky. That put it roughly five feet from the corner the boys were peeking around. He pulled the trigger and shouted at the same time.

Nancy watched as the two boys jumped, scrambled, fell, ran and then leaped over the barbed wire fence. One didn't quite clear and grabbed at his arm, but kept on running. She put on a robe and ran downstairs to find her parents enjoying the spectacle, and laughing so hard that tears ran from their eyes. When they all three calmed down, Nancy thought for a moment then said, "I'm never going to let them forget this night." The laughter started again.

We made the trip to the railroad tracks in record time. There were trips and falls in the darkness, but there was no snake in the world that would have been quick enough to bite us. When we reached the railroad tracks we stopped, panting heavily. We caught our breaths and started walking down the tracks towards town. We walked a ways without saying a word, and then we began to hear the laughter back at Nancy's house. We began to laugh, and laughed so hard that we had to sit on the rails to recover.

We started, again, on our long walk back to town. I reached down and touched the cuts on my arm. It was worth it, I said. Bruner was quiet for a few steps, and then said, " We sure as hell got our excitement." We giggled all the way back to town.

With or Without

This wonderful and awful place
we live in
will continue
with or without
you and I
into a future
we are unable to imagine
because we cannot remember
our past.

The stones
are not still,
continents change shape
a distant rumble
beneath our feet.

Biological families come and go
tribes and clans and peoples
are here and then not
the laughter of happiness
heard over centuries
the quiet or noisy living and dying of
animal, fish and fowl
are mixed into
the murmur of the past
and whispers of the future.

Galaxies spiral,
stars cool and blink out,
stellar gases mix and mingle and glow,
asteroids, meteors, and comets

quietly rumble
through the coldness
and the dusts.

In the blink of an eye
we share what is called now.
There must be a balance
between what was, what is,
and what comes,
lest we miss
our opportunity
to contribute
to what might be
and fall into
what could have been.

We have the greatest of freedoms.
Ours is the choice,
to pass through this world unnoticed,
or noticed,
with or without contentment
with or without fame
with or without peace and love.
with or without
tracks.

www.ingramcontent.com/pod-product-compliance
Lightning Source LLC
Chambersburg PA
CBHW072012170626
46813CB00005B/2130